Must See to Appreciate

Adventures of a Palm Springs Realtor

D. G. VODA

Brown & King Publishers Los Angeles

ATTENTION BOOKSELLERS:
*Wholesale copies of this book may be ordered from
industry distributors Ingram (800-937-8200) and
Baker and Taylor (908-541-7000)*

ISBN: 0615650651
ISBN-13: 978-0615650654
3.1_r7

PRAISE FROM READERS

"An absolute joy! Kept me up all night laughing." —*Patricia McGarry*

"I heard such rave reviews about this book from my friends, I decided to read it... The characters seem so real that I feel these are PEOPLE THAT I KNOW!" —*Flannigan*

"I was sad when there was no stories left to read... The stories are funny because life is funny, and that makes you laugh inside and smile outside. Well done!" —*Christopher Jacob*

"HILARIOUS AND THOUGHT-PROVOKING. I absolutely loved this book. The humor is wonderful—often muted, bubbling just below the surface until something so outrageous happens that you can't help but laugh out loud." —*gbo2486*

DEDICATION

For agents everywhere, in the crossfire

CONTENTS

1   A Buyer Grows Cold   1

2   A Taxing Encounter   23

3   High Tea at the Smoke Tree Ranch   49

4   The Two Natalies Buy a Home   67

5   The Las Palmas Listing   83

6   You're Fading Out   125

ACKNOWLEDGMENTS

Special thanks to David Cantwell, Bob Bennion, Bob Deville, and Susan Zazetti.

[A BUYER GROWS COLD]

D. G. Voda

There is a universal belief among real estate agents that a successful agent must drive a luxurious car. The theory seems to be that prospects will somehow confuse the car's status with the agent's competence, and hence be drawn into his sphere of influence. A Realtor's car, in other words, is a very expensive rabbit's foot, and in the year 2002, the Windsong Palm Springs' parking lot overflowed with Mercedes, BMWs, Cadillacs, Range Rovers, Lincolns, Infinitis, Jaguars, and even (for an agent who advertised that she possessed "A Special Touch of Class") a six-year-old Bentley.

Paula Cooper-Price, her credit destroyed in her recent divorce, couldn't even get in on the ground floor of this automobile arms race. She drove a five year old Nissan Altima that practically screamed, in real-estate-agent-language, "I'm a big zero." Paula told herself that the car was perfectly functional and tried to compensate for its blandness by keeping it immaculately clean, but she was not immune to Realtor superstition. A newly-minted agent with rent to pay and a son to support, she lived from commission to commission, which was one of the reasons she hadn't been able to replace the car, or even, truth be told, make necessary repairs.

She had had a car-shame attack just that morning, when she was getting the Altima smogged at the Shell station on Indian Canyon. The mechanic, a stout, dark-haired guy named Linky if his name tag was to be believed, called her over from the office when he put the car on the dynamometer.

"Your tires are shot," he said matter-of-factly. "But we got a deal this week on Affinity HPs."

Paula couldn't afford to get taken and was instantly suspicious. "They look okay to me," she said.

Linky squatted down and inserted a penny into a groove on the tire, marking the depth of the tread with his fingernail. "Less than a sixteenth-of-an-inch," he said, showing her the coin.

"Is that bad?" Paula asked.

"Lady, you drive on these, you're going to get yourself killed."

Paula felt herself turning red. After the smogging, she hardly had enough left for groceries, let alone tires. But then she was embarrassed that she was embarrassed and angry with Linky for putting her on the spot.

"Just the smog," she said, promising herself to get the tires changed soon.

All of which was why, when she met David Reyes, she really, really, really needed to make the sale.

* * *

David Reyes and his girlfriend had blown into the open house on a whim, but when they started getting serious Paula had maneuvered them pool side, where, stretched out on the trendy lounge chairs, they couldn't help be impressed by the desert vista.

"What do you think?" Reyes said, his hand resting lightly on his girlfriend's blue-jeaned thigh.

"It's okay," said the girl.

"I hate L.A. It's all business. This will be a great weekend place," the actor said.

"It's got a big fenced yard for your dog," Paula prodded.

"Yeah, Doobie will love it," he said. "We can relax here." In his orange watch cap, ripped long-sleeved tee and nylon work-out pants, Reyes looked nothing like the investigator he played on *Cleveland, D.O.A.*, and the girl, Dora Brown, seemed more like an overwrought beautician than a Hollywood bimbo.

"I think it's stupid," Dora said. "All our friends, they'll just want to hang around and get high."

"No, no, just you and me," David Reyes said. "It'll be like a hideout. A safe zone." He turned to Paula. "Dora and me, the reason we're down here is we're swearing off junk. Kicking cold. What's it been now, babe?"

"I don't know," Dora said. "Six hours? What time did we get up?"

"We're through with it," Reyes proclaimed. "That's why I love this house. It's clean, like us. It has a vibe."

"I'm starting to feel a little sick," Dora said.

"You'll see," he said. "Paula here is going to save us. We're going to buy this clean house and have a clean life. It'll be..." he searched for the word, then shrugged and simply repeated– "...clean."

"Let's go back to the hotel," said Dora.

"Relax," Reyes said.

But the girl fidgeted, picking at the fabric of her embroidered silk shirt. Usually it was the woman who developed an emotional attachment to the house and the man who could care less, but in this instance the roles were reversed. Maybe it was a celebrity thing, or a drug thing, or a celebrity drug thing.

It puzzled Paula, but she wasn't going to fret over it. Strike While the Iron is Hot. Reyes wanted the house and he was the one who would be writing the check. She gathered up her big handbag and stood.

"So, shall we write up your offer?"

"How long is that going to take?" said the girl.

"Not long," Paula said. "It's just a few papers."

"Come on, babe," Reyes said, extending his arm. "Business first."

The girl acquiesced and rose. "We'll wait in the car," she said.

At the mention of "car," Paula realized she had a problem.

* * *

Paula moved through the house, locking doors and windows, her mind racing.

She had stupidly violated the first rule of *The $100K Realtor*—always have a contract handy—and now she was going to have to get the clients back to the Windsong office to write up the offer.

But the whole deal was an impulse buy—Reyes had fallen in love with the Buddha shrine in the garden outside the master bedroom—and if Paula let the couple drive back in their own car, Dora's lack of enthusiasm might cause second thoughts. It was dangerous to let them ride together without Paula along to counter objections.

No. Somehow the couple was going to have to ride with her, in her shame-mobile. The other thing was, she wasn't used to dealing with celebrity junkies and sensed that the faster she could get the offer written up the better. Six hours off heroin just didn't seem that long to her.

To make matters worse, there was her 13 year old son Michael. He was home alone today, grounded after being caught by the police drinking at a keg party in Desert Hot Springs. He of course claimed he had had only one beer but his voice had been slurred when the cops had dropped him off. They were supposed to have a long talk when she got home.

She dialed him on the landline. To her relief, he actually picked up, which meant so far he was accepting his punishment.

"What are you doing?" she asked.

"Not getting drunk if that's what you mean," he said.

"Michael," she said.

"I'm watching basketball, okay?"

He had been turning into a smart-ass ever since they got to Palm Springs; that was another part of the conversation they were going to have.

"I might be a little late," she said. "I've got a client."

"That's nice," he said.

"He's a t.v. star," she said.

"Right."

"I'll tell you about it tonight."

"Whatever," he said, and hung up.

* * *

In the garage, where she had parked her hateful Altima, Paula paused and screwed up her determination. Then she pressed the button which opened the garage door and walked outside.

David Reyes and Dora Brown were already seated in their car, a sleek black Porsche 911 two-seater. The car's audio system thumped with a heavy rap beat, the lyrics rhyming "my two fists" with "white Jew bitch." Reyes, at the wheel, turned the volume down as Paula came up to the window.

"We'll just follow you," Reyes said.

"No, no," said Paula. "If we all go in my car we can iron out some of the details, get you back here faster."

"David, the hotel," said the girl, her voice a half-whine-half-warning. Paula feared and hated her.

"I can drop you if you like," Paula said.

The girl looked at Reyes over her sunglasses.

"We'll be fine," said Reyes, squeezing Dora's thigh.

He got out of the car and blooped the alarm, squinting against the desert light into the darkness of the garage, trying to get a look at Paula's car.

Paula quickly crossed in front of him to interpose herself in his line of sight.

"My, umm, husband has the, uh, Bentley," Paula said, turning the key to spring the locks. The Altima didn't even have a blooper.

The girl stood stock still at the edge of the car, clutching her tasseled leather purse.

"Just get in," said the actor.

They each took a seat in the back, leaving Paula to drive, like a chauffeur.

* * *

"How much further?" the girl asked, as they rode along a sandy stretch of the Interstate on the outskirts of Rancho Mirage.

"A few miles," said Paula. The girl's constant interruptions were making it difficult to Develop Empathy with the Client and to Elicit Qualifying Information–techniques she was trying to practice from *The $100K Realtor*, the latest addition to her self-help shelf. Years earlier, growing up in her grandmother's sun-dappled house in Troy, Ohio, Paula had wanted to become a doctor, so that she could push broken bones back into place and pump poison out of the stomach of people who took too much medicine. It proved easier to get pregnant, however, than to master Bio 101 Intro to Life, and there followed in quick succession marriage, a child, Houston, San Diego, betrayal, depression, and divorce. Now, at 36, Paula was starting over. Real estate wasn't doctor-ing, but it could be, occasionally, a living.

At least this offer seemed to be a slam dunk.

"If I paid all cash do you think we could close by the Oscars?" the actor asked. "It'd be fun to have a little barbeque, get some of the guys down here."

"No way," Dora jumped in, before Paula could answer. "You said you and me."

Just then, there came a loud *whump* from the right front fender and Paula knew immediately that her car-shame had caught up to her. The car pulled to the right as she hit the brakes and swerved to avoid a pickup loaded with plastic-covered mattresses. More whumps emanated from the wheel well, forcing Paula to a halt along the side of the road.

She got out of the car and stood on the sandy berm. Reyes and Dora joined her and together they stared at the pathetically deflated tire.

"Ha ha, we have a little flat," Paula said, as if the tire were a disappointing soufflé.

"Do you have a spare?" asked Reyes.

"In the trunk," said Paula. "I'll just call Triple A."

"Christ, look, it's bald," the girl said.

"Just cool it, Dora. You're getting on my nerves," Reyes said to her.

"We should have taken our car," Dora said.

"My car, you mean. I can't even get you to throw out your trash."

Paula stood off to the side of the road, cell phone to her ear, trying to talk to the AAA operator.

"You used to be fun," she heard Dora say to Reyes. "Now you just want to, like, control me."

"Control you? When have I ever been able to control you?"

"You dragged me down here. I just wanted to stay home and work on my album."

"Stay home and get high with Tod Goldberg is more like it," he said.

"At least Tod's fun. He respects my work."

"Respects what's between your legs, you mean."

"You are such an asshole!" said Dora.

Reyes grabbed Dora by her thin arm. "I don't care," he said. "Just don't lie about it."

"Let go of me."

Paula snapped shut the cell phone and ran over, trying to think of a way to restore sanity to the situation.

"Come on, guys," she scolded, sounding more like her high school home-room teacher Mr. Thiruvengadam than a $100K Realtor.

The couple ignored her.

"Just get in the car, Dora."

"No," said the girl, struggling to free herself from his grip.

"Get in the God-damned car!" he said.

He tried to shove her in through the open door, but Dora grabbed the frame and launched herself past him, running down the shoulder of the highway into a sandy ditch, where she promptly fell.

"Where do you think *you're* going?" Reyes taunted.

The girl glared at Reyes with venomous eyes, then, without saying a word, picked herself up and started across the desert scrub. In the distance, a mile away, a tall bronze building stood shimmering in the heat at the edge of town. This was the Laughing Waters Indian Casino, and Dora headed there, clambering across a stony arroyo.

"She'll never make it in those mules," Paula said. She could see that the heels were sinking into the loosely packed soil.

Reyes only grunted, his arms crossed. They watched as she attempted to climb an embankment out of the dry stream bed. As she neared the top, the sand broke loose and sent her sliding to the bottom again. She tried the climb several times before giving up and lying in a crumpled heap at the arroyo's edge.

"Aren't you going to go after her?" Paula finally asked.

"She'll be back for her purse," the actor said.

When Paula looked skeptical, he reached into the backseat, pulled out Dora's handbag, and opened it.

Aside from the usual girly cosmetics, it contained spoons, lighters, hypodermic needles and a handful of little waxed bags, like the kind stamp collectors use, each bearing a cartoon devil logo and the word, "Hell."

Paula looked at the packets with interest. She hadn't realized that heroin was branded.

"I should have dumped her a long time ago," David Reyes said.

* * *

Dora Brown, a quarter mile away, was curled up in a ball on the sand. Paula squinted, trying to see what she was doing. The sun was brutal, and the girl was obviously sick.

Cursing, she grabbed some bottled water from her trunk.

"I'll be right back," she called to the actor, who had withdrawn entirely into the Altima's back seat.

Ten minutes later, dripping with sweat, her practically new Roberto Cavalli top in tatters, Paula reached the prostrate form.

From a distance, the girl appeared lifeless, but when Paula got within a few yards of her, she saw that Dora's eyes were open. Sand stuck to her face where she had been crying. Paula offered a water bottle.

"Come on, get up," Paula said. "You can't stay out here."

"I never slept with Tod Goldberg, I swear," said the girl. "He's just... insightful, that's all."

"I know, I know," said Paula. The sleeve of the girl's shirt was undone, revealing ugly red tracks. "How long have you been doing that?" Paula asked.

"Too long," said the girl. Then she sat up more alertly. "Oh my God, my purse," she said.

"Your purse is safe," said Paula. "Your boyfriend has it."

The girl stood up, sand clinging to her dark jeans. "You don't understand," she said. She brushed past Paula and started running toward the car.

* * *

Paula watched her as she scrambled back up the arroyo, feeling no urgency to follow. *So much potential and yet so screwed up*, she thought.

She let the girl get all the way to the car before she herself stood and started back, wondering what it would be like to be a junkie. Her ex-husband liked to drink and now it looked like Michael was following suit, but drugs had no fascination for Paula, not that they weren't everywhere in Troy when she was growing up.

She passed a giant creosote bush, and stopped in the shadow to breathe in its pungent aroma. With all the drama and delays, there was little chance of writing a deal now. She didn't even have the actor's phone number or email so she could call him when he went back to L.A. She'd have to ask for a card.

She approached the highway and scrambled up the shoulder a hundred feet from the car. Triple-A still hadn't arrived, but she could see some kind of movement in the back seat of the car, a head swaying in a strangely rhythmic fashion, mechanically, like one of those bobbing-head dolls.

Were they–???

God damn them, she thought, unable to understand how one minute they could be tearing at each other like hyenas and the next be doing the nasty in her back seat.

Then, as she got closer, she saw the bare foot extending out onto the pavement. She dropped her water bottle and ran to the vehicle.

Inside, Dora Brown held in her lap the lifeless torso of David Reyes, actor. It was *his* foot that Paula had seen dangling from the car, bare, a hypodermic needle still sticking between the toes. His striped workout pants, so hip and casual, had soaked with urine as his muscles relaxed in death, but Dora held him to her and rocked, oblivious.

"We were supposed to be helping each other, see, doling it out," Dora said, looking up mournfully at Paula. "He couldn't go back to rehab or they'd drop him from the show."

Gently, Paula reached down and pulled the needle from between Reyes's toes, throwing it into the desert with a shudder.

"Come on," said Paula. "You're getting all dirty." She helped the girl slide out from under the body and held her until the tow truck, and then the police, arrived.

* * *

Reyes' picture was all over the newspapers, and Paula was deluged with requests for interviews, even offered payment. The only remarks she made, however, were those she gave to the police. These eventually found their way into the tabloids, along with a photo of Paula they had downloaded from her Windsong website. The girl, Dora Brown, spent a night at Palm Oasis Regional before being transferred to the chemical dependency unit of Glendale Hospital in Los Angeles. She was described as "a frequent club-goer and aspiring musician."

Her son Michael was, for once, impressed. "You're famous, Mom!" he had exclaimed, when her name was mentioned on *E! Entertainment*, and he kept pumping her for details about the incident every night over dinner, hardly even complaining about his confinement for the beer party incident.

* * *

It was almost a week before Paula could get someone from Reyes' agency to come down and claim his car, and when they did, they sent a pair of interns in ripped cargo shorts and carefully-faded polos. The Porsche was still parked in the drive of the Desert Breeze house and she met them there at the agency's insistence to sign a receipt.

"Thanks," said Neil, the tall one with the cropped hair. He had duplicate keys to the Porsche and was going to drive; the other, with the glasses, had wandered away while he and Paula were talking and was now poking his head into the back of the Altima, which was parked at the curb with the windows open.

"Hey dude look at this," he said, staring at the stain where David Reyes had died. Paula's car had been impounded after the incident and she had only gotten it back an hour before.

"Get out of there," Paula said sharply.

Neil ignored her and sauntered up to stand beside his friend. "*Phwew*," he said, peering into the back seat. "How are you going to get *that* clean?"

Paula rubbed her temples. She had been wondering that herself.

———◆———

[A TAXING ENCOUNTER]

Paula Cooper-Price hated her annual visit to the tax man. There was something about pawing through her past—the crumpled receipts, the torn stubs of commission checks, the advertising bills from the *Desert Sun* and *Palm Springs Homes*—that made her feel hollow inside, or rather, made the hollowness inside her resonate, like a gong struck with a wooden mallet.

She was feeling it now, vibrating inside her, as she sat across from J. Michael McManus, C.P.A. Slight of build, red of hair, J. was barely five years out of college and conducted his business out of a tiny office above a Ben & Jerry's in downtown Palm Springs. Paula had first become his customer in the hope that a young, inexperienced accountant would be more inclined to take chances than a C.P.A. who had been around the block a few times. But no. J. was a straight shooter who said, only half in jest, that his job was to keep her out of jail.

"The bottom line is," J. announced, scrolling rapidly through her virtual tax form on the shiny big LCD screen that was the room's only extravagance, "you owe, let's see, $14,321. And three cents, to be exact."

"14,000?" Paula repeated in disbelief. "I can't pay that. What about all those quarterly checks I sent?"

J. pushed back from his desk and balanced himself on the back two legs of his chair. "That's just it, Paula. You only made one quarterly and a portion of another. I called you about that, remember? Plus you missed two payments on your payment plan from last year and that triggered penalties totaling"–he glanced at the screen–"$1,912."

"Jesus!" said Paula.

"I warned you," said J., staring at her steadily through the watery lens of his John-Lennon-style glasses. Was it her imagination or was it pity she read in his eyes?

"Can't we just, like, add a few more deductions?" Paula said after a moment.

"You've already been through one audit," he said, "I wouldn't get too creative in that department, if I were you."

"Well, I can't pay," Paula said. "What do you advise?"

"Do you have any commissions coming?"

"No."

"Can you get a loan?"

"With my credit?"

"Can you sell some jewelry or something?"

"Right."

"How about a partial payment—say $10,000?"

"I could do maybe a thousand," Paula offered, trying to remember how much was left in her savings account.

J. sighed and brought his chair down so it stood on all four legs again. "I guess that will have to do," he said. "Sign here and leave the check."

Paula scribbled her signature on the tax form and, without reading the balance in the register, wrote a check payable to Internal Revenue Service for One Thousand and

00/100 Dollars. Then she rose and made for the door.

"One other thing," J. said, before she could escape.

"What?" Paula said. Against her intent, the word came out petulantly.

"It's not often I advise this, but... I think you should get out of real estate."

"Get out of real estate?" she said. "What else would I do?"

"Paula, you're losing money," J. said, nodding toward the file on his desk. "And at an ever-accelerating rate."

"The market's been slow this year, that's all," said Paula.

"Just think about it," the accountant said, closing her file.

Paula laughed a little laugh of acknowledgment, as if he were making a joke, and stepped out into the corridor, the gong sounding repeatedly in her gut.

On the street, the April sun burned down through the blue desert sky like some science fiction Death Ray, baking the parked tourist buses and etching black shadows in the entries to the stylish shops. The little resort of Palm

Springs had undergone a renaissance in the early years of the new century, its 60's-style World's Fair architecture once again in vogue among the hipsters and tastemakers. Paula had moved here after the divorce because it was cheap and stayed because, at least until recently, real estate was booming. Dozens of agents in the Windsong office were making over a $100,000 a year and Paula had gotten her license on the theory that there was no reason she couldn't be one of them.

Mulling over what J. had said, she walked toward the canopied entrance to the Spa Resort Casino, where her car was parked. Her first full year as a Realtor, Paula had made nine sales, enough to support herself and her son Michael and to make a down-payment on a fixer-upper she intended to remodel and eventually sell. The second year, however—when her plan called for eighteen sales—she again closed nine deals, albeit at a slightly higher dollar volume. Deciding that the problem was marketing, she doubled her advertising budget and even put a few of her listings on the cable channel real estate showcase, at great expense. By then, however, the market had started to turn. Her sales, instead of going up, declined, and the numbers in her bank account followed.

That started her on a cycle of rigid economizing. She dropped the TV exposure and only placed ads in the *Desert Sun* when she had saleable listings. She abandoned the renovations, made her son cut the lawn and trim the bushes, and stopped contributing altogether to her IRA. Nonetheless, her expenses continued to outrun her income, leading to her current impasse with Uncle Sam.

Maybe she should quit real estate. It wasn't like the idea of leaving the business had never crossed her mind before, though usually when frustrated with a deal or burnt out over some difficult client. She had worked for a while in Dallas as a medical transcriptionist; maybe she could go back to doing that.

She reached her car. While she was looking for her keys, the doors to the casino burst open and excited voices wafted out on an air conditioned breeze. There were bells inside too, happy bells, electronic dings and dongs that felt nothing like the ominous toll of the gong in J.'s office.

What the hell, she thought, veering toward the casino doors. *Maybe I'll get lucky.*

* * *

A few hours later and sixty dollars lighter, Paula rose from the BUCK$ AHOY! progressive video slot and headed for the ladies' room, the location of which wasn't immediately apparent among the jangling slot machines, crowded blackjack tables, and spinning roulette wheels. While she had been punching buttons and chatting with the elderly woman beside her, Paula had forgotten her troubles, but navigating the floor of the casino she felt once more adrift. She was trying to remember the name of the client who worked at the Tom Mix Medical Center.

She paused for a minute to watch the action at a craps table near the center of the floor, where a happy, frenetic, and drunken band of gamblers hooted and hollered over the throw of the dice.

"Eight, eight, come on, eight!" the lithe blond woman standing in front of her was shouting. She tossed. The dice danced down the green felt, hopped off the wall and came up eight, prompting groans from half the table while the other half clicked and clucked like excited dolphins. The woman joked with the man to her right, gathered up the chips shoved at her by the stickman and turned, almost knocking over Paula, who was standing slightly behind her and who now, seeing the woman's face, recognized her as Jill Spiegel, her ex-husband's new wife.

Paula's first instinct was to turn and run, before one of Jill's barbs caught in her flesh and tore, but surprise overtook prudence (Jill and Dale lived in San Diego) and she blurted, "My God, what are you doing here?"

"Just hanging," Jill said, holding up her hands to show the chips she had just won. Paula couldn't help but notice the delicate white gold of her wedding ring, so much more elegant than the ring Dale had once given her. "How about you?"

"I'm on my way out," Paula said. Jill was the second or third woman Dale had dated after their divorce and so had nothing to do with their breakup, but some irrational part of her felt that Dale had married Jill as a reproach to her. Jill, after all, was the successful owner of several Mr. Cell Phone kiosks, and, according to Dale (as filtered through Paula and Dale's son) still knew how to party.

Jill hesitated, then said, "Do you have time for a drink?"

"Not really," said Paula. She didn't want to seem unfriendly but Jill had never evinced any particular interest in making conversation before.

"Dale's not here, if that's what you're thinking. I just want to talk."

Paula, always sensitive when the subject of her ex-husband came up, caught a faint undertone in Jill's statement—distress or bitterness, she wasn't sure which. She leapt to what seemed to her the appropriate conclusion. "Oh, are you guys breaking up?" she said.

An annoyed look crossed Jill's face. "No," she said, dropping her casino chips from one hand to the other. When she looked up again the annoyance had turned to anger: "I can't believe you said that."

"I'm sorry," said Paula.

"Well," said Jill, "Dale warned me you were mean."

"Well," said Paula, "Tell Dale to go fuck himself."

In the restroom a minute later, Paula dabbed tears from the corner of her eyes and looked at herself in the mirror. What she saw was a moderately attractive middle-aged woman with too-thick hips and severe lips constrained into a permanent frown. She pushed her skin back at the temples to try to envision the results of the face lift she sometimes thought about. The frown came up a bit and the lines around her eyes disappeared, but when she tried to smile, her nose flared unflatteringly at the base.

If she could have one do-over in her life it would have been marrying Dale Price. She had been so hurt and confused when she discovered he was carrying on an affair with the sexual harassment trainer at the union hall that she stopped eating and required a regimen of Zoloft, Lorazepam, and Ambien just to function. Only the idea that she had to provide a semblance of a normal environment for her son kept her from slicing her wrists. That and *Bejeweled*, the video game that she played endlessly, watching gems fall from the sky. All during the proceedings, while Dale swilled beer at TGIF with his girlfriend and brother electricians, Paula struggled to pay the mortgage and keep the utilities running. When the house was finally foreclosed upon and the Sheriff was sealing the doors, she heard the tolling bell for the first time. She knew in her heart that God had it in for her, and that whatever she set her hand to was destined to crumble to dust, be it marriage or real estate.

Beth Hicken. That was the woman who worked at Tom Mix. She'd call her tomorrow and see whether hospitals still used medical transcriptionists, or if that work had been outsourced to Bangladesh.

* * *

"Paula, we've been over this before. You're just not making your numbers."

The scene was the Windsong Real Estate's manager's office. The *dramatis personae* were Paula Cooper-Price and Lee Kidwell, the Windsong broker. Paula had forgotten that it was time for her bi-annual review.

Kidwell wasn't exactly Paula's boss, since technically she was an independent contractor working for Windsong, but on the other hand agents Kidwell wanted gone eventually went. And with her two years of weak sales, Kidwell wanted to show Paula the door.

"Lee, you know what happened. I can't help it if my last three buyers got cold feet."

"You say here"–he waved the form on which Paula had submitted her semi-annual sales goals–"that you would list six properties by March 31. You listed one."

"That Joey Tyson moved into my farm," Paula protested. "He's got those color jumbo postcards and has his assistants sending handwritten notes."

"Why aren't you mailing color jumbo postcards and sending handwritten notes?" Kidwell asked. Paula was silent. He threw down her sales goals in disgust. "Look, have you ever considered moving to Muffa Realty?"

Muffa was the valley's downscale real estate firm, handling everything from manufactured homes to lots so far out in the desert that you needed GPS coordinates to find them. "Come on, Lee, that's ridiculous."

"Is it?" Kidwell said. "I hear they give their agents lots of support, sales training, telephone scripts..."

"I'm not selling *trailers*," said Paula.

"The problem is, you're not selling much of anything," said Kidwell. "At the very least I'm going to have to give your cubicle to Arnold. He's listed three homes in the last week."

"Fine," said Paula.

It wasn't fine but what was she supposed to do? She knew she didn't have to go right away, but she tromped back to her cubicle and began removing her personal memorabilia–the Magic 8 Ball she used to make decisions, the Prosperity and Wealth voodoo doll she had picked up in New Orleans, the photos of Michael on his snowboard and Grandma in the garden at Troy. She found an empty copy paper box in the Xerox room and carried the stuff to the trunk of her car. Then she got out her phone and called Beth Hicken. There were no golden parachutes in real estate. If she was leaving the business she needed a job, and she needed it fast.

* * *

The Tom Mix Medical Center was a sprawling complex of buildings sandwiched between the Marriott Sun River Resort to the north and the Sultan of Brunei's monstrous purple estate to the south. In the 20s and 30s, Mix had made a string of westerns in the desert, some, like *Trail of Terror* and *Paws and Hooves*, still available at the $9.99 DVD rack. Snapping up cheap acreage, Mix operated a successful dude ranch for many years before his death. The hospital that rose on the former ranch site maintained a hacienda feel and was much favored by aging politicians and movie stars for its excellent cardiology and plastic surgery units.

Lately the hospital was also known for Serenity, the chemical dependency rehab facility that had hosted the likes of Tom Sizemore and Kirstie Alley. It was here that Beth Hicken worked as a rehabilitation therapist. She remembered Paula, didn't seem at all surprised to hear from her, and made a slot in her apparently busy schedule to see her at two p.m. without inquiring about the nature of her visit. Only after Paula hung up did the possibility occur to her that Beth probably thought Paula wanted to check herself in.

The clinic itself was at the far corner of the property, hemmed in on one side by the Sultan's purple wall and on the other by a parking lot and a tall hedge of oleander. Paula followed the signs between the rows of cute bungalows and within minutes found herself sitting in Beth Hicken's office, in the corner of the large central community building done up in a breezy Santa Fe style.

"Thanks for seeing me on the spur of the moment," Paula said, sitting in a cushy club chair across from Beth's desk. She indicated the landscaped view out the window beside her. "This isn't what I expected."

"We try to make our clients comfortable," Beth said. "Can I get you some coffee?"

"No thanks," said Paula. "How are you liking your house?"

"We love it," said Beth. "You'll have to come by and see it now that it's decorated." She eyed Paula through her thick glasses. "But you didn't come here to discuss real estate."

"Not exactly," said Paula. "Although that plays into it."

"It does?" said Beth.

"I'm not here for myself," Paula said hastily, thinking she better make clear that she didn't want to be admitted as a patient.

"Of course not," said Beth. "I understand."

"You do?"

"Do you keep in close touch with your husband?"

Paula was confused. She usually was mum about her personal life with clients, though it wasn't impossible she might have mentioned her divorce at some time while touring houses with Beth.

"Not very close," Paula admitted. "Although I ran into his new wife Wednesday at the casino."

"Yes, she mentioned that."

"What?"

"She mentioned that she ran into you. But she didn't say you were coming to visit."

"She's here?"

"Not now. But you'll be able to see Dale in," she glanced at a wall clock, "well, now, if we hurry. He's only got ten minutes between meetings." She stood. "He's in the Liza Minnelli room. I'll show you the way."

Paula sat for a moment, unable to pick herself out of her chair as she waited for the swirl of contradictory feelings to settle. Dale in rehab? She could hardly believe it. Not because he didn't belong there–Paula had long endured his bouts of drunkenness and fretted over the increasing amounts of Vicodin he took "for back pain"–but because Dale was so arrogant that she couldn't imagine him asking for help. Even when he drove the truck into a telephone pole he claimed to be dodging a turtle (turtle!), even though his blood alcohol level was .13. For Dale, everything was someone else's fault.

There was no way she wanted to see him now. They would only get into an argument (she had been asking him to send over her vacuum attachments for three years now), and he would throw in her face the restraining order she had been forced to get and then they would be right back at it, trading injuries tit-for-tat and shredding each other with hateful names that would, independently, cause each to wake up in the middle of the night calling down curses on the other's head.

She was about to explain all this to Beth Hicken, who, smiling, was holding the door to the office open, unaware she had taken a blowtorch to Paula's soul. But in the corridor a woman with a wheeled yellow bucket was mopping a spill off the floor, and the strong scent of bleach hit Paula like a slap. Suddenly

Paula was afraid, but more for Dale than for herself. People died of drugs and alcohol. She had better find out if he were okay.

* * *

Dale was neither hanging out with the other addicts in the meeting room nor sitting in the atrium beneath the big TV tuned to "Cheers." Paula found him outside, alone on a concrete bench in the desert-landscaped garden, smoking a cigarette. His arms were on his thighs, as if his torso were too heavy to hold up, and he was staring at a point just beyond the tip of his shoe, a target for his flicked ashes. He had a three-day growth of beard, his hair was mussed, and when he looked up at Paula, there were dark crescents below his eyes.

"Come to see the freak show?" he said, bitterly, then, before she could reply, said, "I'm sorry. I'm such an asshole."

There were lots of things Paula could have said to that but he looked so haggard she didn't have the heart. "How are you doing?" she asked.

"Okay," he said, "except that I haven't slept in a week and everyone here is a crystal meth addict. I have to go to five meetings a day and all they talk about is Higher Power this and Higher Power that." He crushed his cigarette on the concrete and then held the filter awkwardly in his hand. "We get demerits if we don't bring in the butts," he explained.

"'Clean up your own messes,'" she said, making a joke of the phrase she had used to nag Dale and Michael the entire time they were a family.

"Something like that," he said, looking a bit sheepish. "I was going to call you. I don't think I'll be out in time to take Michael next weekend."

"That's okay," said Paula.

"He already hates me so I don't think it will make much difference."

"He doesn't hate you," said Paula. "He just doesn't get enough of you."

Dale's mouth tightened in a familiar expression of anger, then relaxed. "You're right," he said. "I shouldn't be so defensive."

"What do you want me to tell him?" Paula asked.

"The truth," said Dale. "That his old man's a drunk and a drug addict and is holed up in a hospital named after a fake cowboy that he's not even sure if his insurance will cover."

"I'll say you're away at a job site," Paula said.

"A job site," snorted Dale.

"If I tell him you're in here he'll just want to come. What's the point of putting him through that? You can talk to him next time you see him, when this is all over."

"You're right, you're right, I'm a selfish prick like they say." He turned to her and took her hand. "How are you, Paula? You doing okay."

She was surprised by the sudden gush of sincerity and wasn't sure if she could entirely trust it. His hands were big and rough and she always liked when he held her hands in his, though she could have done without the smelly cigarette butt crushed against her skin. "I'm fine," she said.

"No, really," he said.

"Really, I'm fine," said Paula. "Except, well, I owe the IRS some money."

"How much?" he said.

"$14,000."

"I'll pay it," he said.

"How are you going to pay it?" Paula asked. "You can't even pay for this."

"I owe you," said Dale.

Paula sighed. Making big promises he'd never be able to follow through on was a typical knightly Dale Price gesture, one of the reasons she had fallen in love with him in the first place. Strangely, although she knew he was blowing smoke and that she would never see a cent, she felt reassured. A Dale making extravagant promises was a Dale who at least believed he'd survive to fight again.

"You don't owe me anything," Paula said.

"Dale, let's go!" called a man in pressed black slacks, one of the counselors, Paula presumed.

Dale rose. "I'll call you," he said.

She doubted it.

Paula lingered in the garden after Dale had gone, watching a hummingbird gather nectar from the blooming ocotillos. *Buzz, buzz, buzz* the little bird went, its wings a blur of prodigious energy as it darted here and there after its sustenance. Surely, Paula thought, it had to be using up more energy than it was getting from the nectar, but there it was, still aloft, maneuvering around the thorns to dip its beak into the tiny red flowers, all the while flapping for dear life. The sight made her feel relaxed and drowsy, and after a while she walked along the garden path until she found herself back at the entry to the clinic.

Here she hesitated, wondering whether she should return to Beth Henley, explain why she had really come to the clinic, and see what she could find out about medical transcriptionists. But after the events of the day it all seemed too overwhelming. She turned in the other direction and walked out into the parking lot, thinking about color jumbo postcards.

* * *

That night, in the wee hours of April 16th, J. Michael McManus arrived home after 18 hours of stomping out tax-deadline fires. At midnight he had dropped the last batch of client tax forms at the Palm Springs post office, then stopped for a double bourbon at Jazz Upstairs to clear his head of the rows of marching numbers. He hated April 15th, hated his clients, and hated accounting in general, a profession he had gotten into because he was good in math and because his father, a partner at Weiss, Hirsch, Rifkin, Page & Simon, had both warned him away from lawyering and ridiculed his idea to move to New York to study musical theater. *Boom.* There was that hollow feeling again, the one in his gut that Dr. Povoledo said was acid reflux, but which seemed stubbornly resistant to Prilosec, Zantac and Tagament.

In his mailbox were the usual flyers from the supermarkets and hardware stores, copies of both *Forbes* and *CPA Magazine*, a keyboard catalog from Andy's Music, and a hand-addressed envelope with a Ronald Reagan stamp and no return address. He threw himself onto his rumpled couch (he had taken to sleeping there of late) and ripped the envelope open.

"Dear Jarlath," it read, in elegant handwriting. *"I hope you're enjoying life at 827 W. Mirada Lane! I'm a Realtor with many recent sales in your area and can sell your home too! Please call me immediately for a free market analysis! Sincerely yours, Joey Tyson"*

J. blinked and read the note over again, trying to make sense of it before finally concluding that it was computerized junk mail cleverly printed to look like personal handwriting. He momentarily held it, wondering if he should pass it on to Paula Cooper-Price, then tossed it on the floor with yesterday's newspapers, feeling sick to his stomach.

————❖————

[HIGH TEA AT
THE SMOKE TREE RANCH]

Paula Cooper-Price almost didn't make it to the high tea at the Smoke Tree Ranch since she had written it in her appointment book wrong and only happened to see the correct date in the Palm Springs Pioneer Society newsletter when she was clearing off her desk at the Windsong office.

The guard at the gatehouse gave her a long and suspicious look, double-checking her drivers license with its horrible photo against a long list of names on the guest list and making a phone call before finally admitting her through the rustic gates. He gave her a map of the complex on which he had highlighted specific driving directions to the clubhouse, correctly assuming she had never been there before.

Paula found the whole idea of high tea at the Smoke Tree Ranch intimidating and would have preferred to be anywhere but here. But she was a real estate agent, which meant that she had to show her face around and get known in the community, especially with the sort of people who hung out over tea at the clubby "ranch."

Besides, there was always a chance that she'd meet someone romantically.

The grounds of the Smoke Tree were a subtle rift on an English garden, done desert-style with sagebrush, palms and flowering cactus, and the rustic "bungalows" were half-hidden off the gravel road and never showed up on any real estate computers at Windsong or anywhere else. The Smoke Tree Ranch was nothing if not private. Paula was here only because she had accidentally become a volunteer at the Pioneer Society museum before she knew who was who in Palm Springs.

The clubhouse was a lodge-like structure with extensive views over the grounds to the mountains. In the foyer she was greeted with a hug by Lily O'Donald, the Pioneer Society President.

"Lily, thank God," said Paula. "Is my camisole slipping?" The neckline of her dress was a little low and Paula didn't want anything showing that wasn't supposed to show at the Smoke Tree Ranch.

Lily had been a hat check girl at the Chi Chi Club before marrying into the horsey set. She was the one person in the Society Paula felt comfortable with.

"No honey, you look fine," she said.

"I love this dress but I can barely fit in it. I'm on that 14 Day Colon Cleansing Juice Fast, you know."

Lily, a woman of now-generous proportions, clucked and stood back to appraise her. "Like you have any weight to lose," she said. She nodded toward the club room, where a mix of older men and woman buzzed around silver trays of tea and cakes. "Come on, let me introduce you to the Scion."

The Scion was Howard Brenner, a 2nd generation Pioneer whose family still owned scores of acres in Palm Springs. Lily, apparently determined to help a fellow striver get ahead, had been threatening to introduce Paula to him. When Paula had protested that someone of his wealth would already know plenty of agents, Lily just smiled and said, "We'll see." From Ellen, another volunteer at the Society, Paula had learned that the Scion was in the middle of a contentious divorce.

Now, feeling light-headed, Paula let herself be dragged through the buzzing crowd and deposited before a thin, precisely-dressed man in horn-rimmed glasses a few years older than herself.

"Howard, Paula. Paula, Howard," Lily chanted, then, to Howard Brenner, "Paula's a real estate agent, you know."

* * *

Lily disappeared, leaving Paula feeling naked and exposed in the scrutiny of Brenner's appraising eyes.

"A real estate agent," Brenner said. "Really?"

Paula felt her face reddening, although she couldn't have said whether from the tone of Brenner's voice or from the flick of his eyes to her somewhat-too-exposed bosom.

She shifted her weight and squirmed in her dress. "It's a job," she said lamely. "It keeps bread on the table." Actually, lately, it didn't. To earn some extra money, she had secretly been helping an agent friend at another company organize her home office.

He raised his eyes to hers and took a sip of tea. "I suppose Lily has been telling tales about me," he said. He was a not-unattractive man, with a full head of hair going gray at the temples and a sun-burnt face. Only his glasses were peculiar.

"I'm not here to solicit your business, if that's what you mean," she said, the blood still rising in her face.

"It's okay," he said. "Both my wives were real estate agents. It's no worse than flogging magazines." The Scion spent most of his time back East running a group of health magazines. He stopped a waiter in a white jacket and had him pour Paula some tea.

"One lump or two?" Brenner said, playfully lifting a lump of raw sugar with a silver claw.

"Uh, one," said Paula, trying not to look at the cookies on the tray.

"You're a very good looking woman," he said, stirring her tea and looking at her innocently through the thick lenses of his glasses.

"I'm married," said Paula, her standard lie to ward off passes.

A dark look crossed his face and he handed her the tea cup perfunctorily and then gazed out over the crowd. "Don't bust my balls," he said.

Paula tried to grab a cookie off the tray as the waiter moved away, but found her hand swimming in the air.

"You... You..." Paula said.

It was her last utterance before Paula fainted dead away.

* * *

Paula awoke on a bench on the patio just outside of the Smoke Tree clubhouse. She was wrapped in Howard Brenner's arms, and Lily hovered over her like a fretful hummingbird.

For the past six days, the only nourishment that had passed her lips had been raw lime and grapefruit juice mixed with a little spring water, although she had cheated on the second day by eating a grapefruit half instead of juicing it. She was trying to lose the eight pounds she had put on over the winter eating dark chocolate almond bark from See's and worrying about how to take care of herself and her kid.

"Are you all right?" Lily said, as Paula regained consciousness. Her head was resting on Brenner's chest, and the first thing she saw was the gold button of his Navy blazer. He smelled faintly of cologne.

She sat up, still a bit woozy. Inside the club Paula could see a clump of Society ladies, tea cups in hand, staring out at her through the big picture window.

"I'm okay," she said. "I just haven't eaten."

"I'll get you something," Lily said, scurrying back inside.

Brenner eyed her appraisingly. "You're not a diabetic, are you?" he inquired. "Laura is diabetic."

Her head cleared a little and she managed to sit up, freeing herself from Brenner's grasp. "Who's Laura?" she said.

"My daughter," Brenner said. "Look at those old coots."

A crowd of blue-haired matrons had gathered at the clubhouse windows; Paula had become the afternoon's entertainment.

"They're all watching," he said. "Let's go over there." He indicated a picnic bench near the croquet court.

"All right," said Paula, angry at herself for making a spectacle.

Brenner smiled and helped her to her feet. She hated being so helpless but her head was still swimming.

"I just need some food," Paula said.

Brenner walked her to the picnic bench and was just sliding in beside her when Lily arrived with a plate of finger sandwiches and cakes.

"Would you like me to call a doctor?" Lily asked.

"No, I'll be okay.," Paula said.

Lily hesitated, and Brenner took the plate from her. "She'll be fine," he said. "Go on back to the party."

"I can sit for a minute," said Lily.

Brenner handed Paula a fork and a little glazed white cake on a napkin.

"She'll be fine," said Brenner firmly to Lily. Lily lingered for a moment and then left them alone.

* * *

Paula had already finished one *petit four* and was starting on another. After almost a week without solid food, the amaretto and almond filling tasted heavenly.

Brenner watched her eat. She tried to appear dainty and refined, but she was famished and cleared the plate like a construction worker.

"I'm sorry," she said. "I'm just very hungry."

He smiled and waited for her to finish. "You have beautiful hands. Has anyone ever told you that?"

Her hands right now were sticky with sugar and, embarrassed, Paula dropped them into her lap. Brenner reached over and took them in his. "No ring," he said, "that's how I knew you weren't married," and she remembered he had been in the middle of making a pass at her when she had conked out.

She had been divorced for over two years now and her love life was as bad as her business. The only man she had been with since her husband was Carter Quinn, a slightly effeminate elementary school teacher from L.A. that she had met while having drinks with a friend at the Village Pub. Carter proved to be anything but effeminate, but then expected to sleep with her any time he visited Palm Springs until she finally told him to stop calling. That had been last fall, before the eight pounds.

Brenner, by contrast, seemed slightly creepy to her with his fat glasses and neatly trimmed hair, but maybe because of Lily's introduction and the sugar now coursing through her brain she couldn't decide whether to encourage or discourage him. Instead, she felt the warmth creeping back into her face and looked down at where his thin brown hands held hers, a schoolgirl surprised by her emotions.

"No ring," Brenner repeated. "And very pretty. Either you're divorced or you have ice water in your veins," he said.

His eyes were brown, and the lens of the glasses made them appear bigger than they were, and at the same time indistinct, like pebbles in a stream bed. "I'm divorced," she said.

"It's difficult, isn't it?"

"What is?"

"Being alone."

"I suppose," said Paula.

"Have you ever been to New York?"

"Why?" asked Paula, a little disturbed by the direction the conversation was taking.

"I'm going to kiss you now, okay?"

His request was so unexpected and direct that before Paula could decide about it his lips were brushing hers. They were dry, cracked lips, and touched hers like a question.

Paula came to her senses and broke away. "I don't think this is such a good idea," she said, removing her hands from his and sliding a few inches down the bench.

"Why not?" he said.

"Well, for one thing, your wife."

"We're separated."

"Look, you're very nice," said Paula diplomatically, "but I just met you."

"What is it? What did Lily say about me?" he demanded.

"I've got to go," Paula said, rising.

She scurried back into the gathering, leaving Brenner sitting at the picnic table looking frustrated.

* * *

When she re-entered the club, there was a moment of silence, then everyone started talking to each other at once, studiously not noticing Paula. When she stooped to pick up a cup from the tea tray, she saw why: the picnic table that had seemed out of sight from the window on the left was directly visible from the window on the right, on the other side of the fireplace. Everyone in the room had seen her let Brenner embrace and kiss her.

There was an awkward moment while Paula stood alone, then Lily excused herself from a group near the entrance and came up to her.

"You're looking a lot better," she said.

"Am I?"

"That didn't go off so well, did it?" said Lily, indicating Howard Brenner, who was still seated on the bench staring off across the empty croquet field to the mountains.

"It was a little unexpected," said Paula. Her dress was riding up at her waist again and she tried to pull it back into place without being too obvious.

"Don't worry about it," said Lily. "He's getting a reputation."

"What do you mean?"

"He's having a second childhood since Phyllis White left him," Lily said. "You handled yourself magnificently."

"Thanks," Paula said. "I guess."

"I thought you guys might hit it off. I hope you don't mind."

"You should have warned me."

"Oh, phoo! You're both adults. What are you waiting for, lightning to strike?"

At the Pioneer Society museum, Paula had come across a picture of Lily, young and slender, being boosted onto a horse by two bandanna-ed cow pokes at some local dude ranch. Now Paula realized that it was no coincidence that there were *two* cow pokes, or that Lily had been going riding in a short tennis skirt.

"If you'll excuse me, I guess I'll be on my way," Paula said, putting down her tea cup.

"Of course," said Lily, feeling the rebuke. "Thank you for coming and here, you missed your gift bag while you were out."

Paula reached into the bag Lily had thrust into her hands and pulled out a dispenser of White Tea and Ginger soap.

"Thank you," said Paula. "It's very nice."

"It foams," said Lily.

Paula felt every eye upon her as she left the room.

She had the car started and the windows down when Brenner came running up the dusty path.

"Listen, I'm sorry," he said, pushing forward his eyeglasses, which were sliding down the bridge of his nose.

"It's okay," Paula said. She really just wanted to get away but he was leaning against her car.

"No, Lily told me I embarrassed you. "That was very crass of me."

Paula had never heard anyone use the word "crass" before in a serious way. "Did she send you here?"

The question momentarily derailed him. "Who?"

"Lily."

"No," he said. "I'm clumsy. I was never any good with women. Men I understand. At least let me make it up to you."

"Make it up to me how?" Paula asked. For a moment she imagined maybe he was about to ask her to list some of his property, although she was instantly ashamed of the money-grubbing thought. On the other hand, if there were money to be grubbed she wasn't in any position to turn it down.

"Why don't you come over to the ranch," he said. "We'll have dinner, maybe go for a swim? I have a nice hot tub we can get into..."

"I don't think so," Paula said. "But thanks for asking." She put the transmission into reverse and waited for him to step back. A hard glint of anger appeared in his eyes, clearly visible through the horn rims.

"You know something?" he said. "You real estate bitches are all the same."

Paula punched the accelerator, sending the car brusquely backwards in a little circle of dust. Then she threw the car into drive and took off down the road toward the Smoke Tree Ranch exit, leaving Howard Brenner, Palm Springs

Pioneer, looking sad and disheveled in the gravel lot in front of the clubhouse.

Real estate bitch, she thought. *He could just go screw himself.* She breezed through the gate with a casual wave to the now-friendly attendant, then, out of sight of the guard house, pulled into the Bank of America parking lot while tears stung her eyes and ruined her makeup. It wasn't so much that she had made a fool of herself or been made a fool, it was that everyone else seemed to have a place and knew where they belonged. She was Ruth, standing amidst the alien corn, if her bible class memory served her correctly.

Oh well, she thought, when she had cried herself out and the tears subsided. At least she had stirred things up a bit.

———✦———

[THE TWO NATALIES BUY A HOME]

D. G. Voda

Woozily, Paula Cooper-Price groped for the light pull in the garage of the Puma-Vista-house-she-couldn't-really-afford and edged around the bulk of the recently-purchased-Land-Rover-she-couldn't-really-afford, looking for the dented metal box containing her half of her former husband's tool collection. She was sick as a dog. Her muscles ached and her brain throbbed. Normally a careful dresser, this morning she wore an old sweat shirt pulled over baggy pajama bottoms and her hair stuck out in multiple directions.

All she cared about right now was finding the damned plumbers wrench.

The deal had come to this: if she could get the water at the Merv Griffin flowing long enough to satisfy the amateur transsexual home inspector, Nasty Natalie would sign the last of the escrow papers and Paula's son could continue another year at the Bull Run Military Academy, where for the first time since Paula's divorce the boy wasn't giving her any lip.

On the other hand, no water, no escrow papers. The transsexual home inspector would pronounce doom, Nasty Natalie would withhold her signature, the whole deal would go up in a flame of law suits, and Paula would be out her well-deserved commission–$15,000, enough to bring up the arrears at Bull Run and tide her through to her next deal, if she fudged on her taxes, and if there was a next deal.

Paula found the toolbox hiding behind some boxes of old escrow papers on the floor under more boxes of broken, supposedly collectible, Fiestaware.

This she lifted, with difficulty, onto the tailgate of the Rover. She checked to make sure the plumbers wrench was indeed inside, then with both hands shoved the heavy toolbox into the cargo area.

She felt like she was going to puke. She steadied herself against the car and bent over with her mouth open, waiting to see if anything would come out. For a moment she doubted that she was strong enough to get in the car and go wrestle with a water valve.

But her commission was in danger, and with it, everything she had worked so hard for.

She hated the two Natalies.

Taking several deep swallows, she pulled herself together. How long could it take to turn a valve?

* * *

The condo was a semi-attached townhome at the Merv Griffin Palm Springs Villas. Theoretically, the buyers had already had their final walk-through. "Nasty Natalie" (Natalie King was her real name) and "Nice Natalie" (Natalie Vacca, her partner) were a lesbian couple who had spent over six hours at the house flushing toilets, running showers and sending food scraps down the garbage disposal, accompanied by a man in a bad wig and Raggedy Ann overalls whom they introduced as their "niece" but who functioned as a know-it-all legal, mechanical and decorative advisor.

That was Tuesday. The escrow was supposed to close Friday. But Thursday morning at 7:57 a.m., an aching, sleep-deprived

Paula had gotten a call on her cell from Scott Drane, the buyers' agent.

"Did you feel the earthquake?"

"What earthquake?" asked Paula.

"Four point nine, centered somewhere near Amboy." Scott hesitated. "My buyers want another walk-through. In case there's earthquake damage."

"You're kidding, right?" Paula said. "Amboy's way out past Twentynine Palms. Fifty miles at least."

Scott, who had been an agent for half his life, sighed a sigh of deep real estate wisdom. Scott hated his clients as much as Paula did–he was the one who had started calling them "Nice Natalie" and "Nasty Natalie"–but was too much of a pragmatist to let mere personalities stand between him and a commission check.

"We're closing tomorrow," he said. "Let's just humor them along."

"But they've already had their walk through," Paula declared.

"I know, I know," said Scott. "I faxed them the papers but they didn't sign off. Now the earthquake's got them spooked."

Paula dragged herself upright and stared out her bedroom window at her front yard, where the automatic sprinkler was drenching the *Desert Sun*. Dealing with Scott's clients was like trying to stuff a large comforter into a small washing machine, and she was exhausted with the effort. No sooner had her seller accepted their offer than Nasty Natalie was trying to back out of it, claiming Paula had tricked her into paying too much and had withheld vital information from her, like the fact that there was a cigarette burn on the guest bedroom carpet under a nightstand. It took Nice Natalie two days to talk her down. And later in the contract period, Nasty Natalie was hysterical again, this time in a snit because, driving by, she had noticed one of the orange trees in the back yard had a broken limb.

Paula's concentration was shot.

"Tell you what," said Scott, in his smoothest real-estate-voice, after her long delay in speaking. "I'll open up and go through with them, pour some balm on their shattered nerves."

"I guess. As long as I don't have to get involved. I'm sick."

"Sorry to hear that. What's wrong?"

"I don't know," said Paula. "Ebola I think. I just can't deal with those two today."

"Don't worry about it," he had said. "You won't ever have to see their faces again, I swear."

But two hours later Scott was on the line. He hated to ask her, but the clients were insisting: the water was off and Paula was the only one who knew how to open the vacation valve.

* * *

Paula, in blue jeans and an old flutter sleeve top, knelt by the side of the road on a scrap piece of cardboard, poking a wrench into dark hole. It was only 11 a.m., but the heat from the asphalt seemed to be roasting Paula's brain inside her skull as she tried first one pair of valves, then another.

"Try it now," bellowed Natalie King, the nasty Natalie, who stood over Paula like a prison guard, hands on hips. Her companion, the Nice Natalie, leaned demurely against Paula's Rover, a big floppy hat protecting her from the broiling desert sun.

"Nothing!" screamed Raggedy Ann, sticking his bewigged head through the little bathroom window on the side of the house. He was inside with Scott Drane, turning the shower knobs as Paula tried the valves.

"Nothing," repeated Nasty Natalie, as if Paula couldn't hear. "I thought you said it was simple."

Paula peered into the mess of valves and cursed under her breath. The vacation valve shut the water off in the resort house when her client, the seller, was away. According to him, all she had to do was open the underground box at the edge of the property and turn the valve. But there were multiple valves in the box and now she couldn't raise the owner on his cell phone, forcing her to try the valves one by one in various combinations. This had been going on now for forty minutes.

Paula, blood pounding, sat back on her heels in defeat.

"I guess we're going to have to call a plumber," she said.

"You're damned right we're going to have to call a plumber," Nasty Natalie replied. "I know exactly what you're trying to do, you know."

"What do you mean?"

"You're keeping the water off trying to conceal the leaks."

"What?"

"You're not fooling me. You came down here bright and early to turn those valves off. Just as soon as you heard about the earthquake."

Paula couldn't believe her ears. "Are you kidding me?" she said, drawing herself upright on her knees.

Nasty Natalie snorted and leaned forward. "I'm onto you honey. You've been trying to cheat us from the very start. You didn't tell us about missing molding, or the stain in the back of the closet, and now you pull this shit with the water. You think I'm stupid? You think I don't know the little game you're playing, pretending you can't work those valves. No way are we closing on this house!"

Paula stood up, light-headed, the blood draining from her sweaty brow, the wrench feeling heavy and hot in her hand. Nasty Natalie was going on and on, but somehow her voice sounded far away, and Paula felt like she was looking at her through a cardboard tube, seeing only the woman's vermillion lips moving and moving in an endless stream of what she knew were loose and crazy accusations, but which she heard as the *bzzzz bzzzz bzzzz* of an angry wasp. Paula felt her arm go up, and then swat down, the wrench missing its mark and smashing the woman's thick neck muscles instead of her blabbing, hateful face.

Nonetheless, the impact had its effect. Natalie King, Paula's last best hope of keeping a roof over her head and her son in school, tumbled over backwards onto the lawn, a huge sack of falling meat.

Paula dropped the wrench in the grass, horrified. She really was sick.

* * *

The Palm Springs Police Department building was a Modernist masterpiece designed by Albert Frey. Even the holding cell where they had stashed Paula after hauling her off from the house had a high horizontal window through which she could admire the peaks of the Santa Rosa mountains. Thousands of tiny trees were silhouetted along the tops of the ridge line, giving the mountains a serrated edge, like a saw blade tearing at the flesh of the sky.

Her bones ached and she wrapped her bare arms around her torso. The polished concrete bench, a shelf jutting out of the glazed brick wall, was too hard to lie on and too square to sit on, so she shifted from one uncomfortable position to the other.

But even as she sat there shivering, she knew she was in big trouble. When she was charged she would have to get a lawyer, her own, not a company lawyer as she doubted the E&O insurance at Windsong Realty covered clobbering buyers with a pipe wrench. There would probably be both criminal and civil cases filed, but maybe she could claim temporary insanity due to the stress of her divorce, even though it was several years ago. She'd have to pull her son out of Bull Run and send him to the local public high school, a fate, she knew, he'd fiercely resist. And what if the Department of Real Estate suspended her license while the court cases were being sorted out? How would she support herself and her son?

She wished she'd never met the two Natalies.

Just then the steel door swung open. Standing there was one of the cops who had taken her into custody.

"You're free to go, mam'n," he said. "There aren't going to be any charges."

Behind him, grinning, stood Scott Drane, his suit rumpled from the pandemonium at the house.

"Come on, client killer," he said with a wink. He held out a hand and helped her off the bench.

Outside on the steps, he stopped and took a close look at her.

"How are you feeling? I can take you to Desert Regional if you want..."

"I'll be all right once I get home," said Paula. "But what happened? I thought my goose was cooked."

Scott paused and lit a cigarette.

"It would have been," he said, "if it wasn't for Natalie--the *other* Natalie, the nice one."

"What do you mean?"

"After the cops took you away the two Natalies got in a fight. It seems Nice Natalie really wanted the house and was pissed that Nasty Natalie was making everything so difficult. One thing led to another and before the cops could pull them apart, Nice Natalie beaned her girlfriend with that pipe wrench of yours. Except her aim was better and they took Nasty Natalie away in an ambulance."

"What happened to Nice Natalie?"

"The cops arrested her. But not before she signed this," Scott said, pulling a tattered paper from his coat pocket. It was the Verification of Final Walk-Through document. "We're home free, baby. Escrow closes tomorrow on schedule."

Paula took the paper and stared at it, trying to focus.

"But they're taking title as Tenants in Common. Don't they both have to sign?"

"That's the beauty of love," Scott said. "They're Registered Domestic Partners. One signature's all we need."

Later that afternoon, when Paula finally awoke from her NyQuil induced coma, she lay in her hot bed listening to the house crack and reflected on the events of the day. The deal was a squeaker but she'd take it. She might still get her butt sued but at least now she'd have a few bucks to defend herself.

She wondered about the transsexual home-inspecting niece. He seemed to have a flair for real estate; maybe he'd be interested in the fixer-upper over at Swaying Palms?

"She." She meant "she."

Her head hurt. Paula reached for the little plastic cup and gulped another shot of NyQuil.

———◆———

[THE LAS PALMAS LISTING]

Paula Cooper-Price was so angry she thought her head would explode.

She had just gotten off the phone with Gordon Fairclough, her prospect from Bucks County, Pennsylvania, who had called to let her know he wouldn't be needing her assistance anymore in finding a Palm Springs home because that wonderful Dionne Searcey woman had faxed him a few listings at the hotel and he and his wife had decided to buy a nice view property in Little Tuscany that had everything they wanted except a salt water pool, and for only $1.8 million—a steal in his estimation.

"Shit," said Paula. "Shit, shit, shit." She slammed her cell phone down so hard that the battery came off and skittered across the floor of the Koffe Klub, whizzing under the table of the two teens across from her, who recoiled in fear when Paula approached to retrieve it.

"Sorry," said Paula automatically, but her thoughts were consumed with that brazen bitch Dionne Searcey, that unethical, greedy, but she-had-to-admit-stylish-and-beautiful piece of Realtor crap who already controlled half the high-end real estate listings in town but who apparently had nothing better to do than steal other agents' clients right out from under them, even when those other agents were barely scraping along and had a living room full of mismatched, cat-shredded furniture which desperately needed to be replaced.

Paula hated Dionne Searcey.

Of course, Lee Kidwell, the broker-manager in her office, would point out that it was Paula's fault that she had been showing properties to a client without a Buyer Broker Representation Agreement, but the Faircloughs had seemed so refined and high-toned that Paula hadn't been able to bring herself to ask them to sign a grubby little legal document until she had proved her worth by locating for them the perfect fabulous vacation home. Apparently

Dionne Searcey had no such qualms, and didn't care that the Faircloughs were a referral from HomeFind.com that cost Paula $95 a lead.

Paula hated Dionne Searcey.

Dionne Searcey was a Palm Springs brand name, one of those highly successful, "top-producer" agents who had her own advertising page in the *Desert Sun*, her own van to haul around clients, and even her own downtown office for her "team" of agents, little Dionne Searcey clones who traipsed after clients fawningly whenever they crossed the threshold of a Dionne Searcey listing. Of these there were myriad, especially in the upscale neighborhoods like Las Palmas, Little Tuscany, and the Movie Colony, where half the homes for sale had a huge-but-elegant Dionne Searcey sign. Dionne Searcey had twice been named "Top Ten Listing & Sales Agent" and had "$81 Million in Closed Sales" last year, according to a press release printed practically verbatim in the *Desert Sun*'s real estate section, which knew which side its bread was buttered on.

Paula's own business amounted to $49,000 in commissions last year, and that was before expenses. Most of her clients could barely afford to live in the area at all, and her most successful farm area was the Sand Pebble, a run-down-but-inexpensive condo development wedged in between the airport and busy Ramon Road. When she wasn't envying Dionne Searcey's wardrobe or dreaming of ramming the side of Dionne Searcey's silver Lexus, Paula had to acknowledge a certain grudging admiration for Dionne Searcey's success. Somehow, starting from nothing just like Paula, Searcey had managed to get a finger hold in the high-end luxury real estate market, and once there had never let go. She had grit.

But Paula had grit, too, or at least believed she did. Starting a year ago, in direct competition with Dionne Searcey, she had boldly launched a farm area in Las Palmas, a venerable Palm Springs neighborhood once populated by the likes of Katherine Hepburn and Mario Lanza but now largely inhabited by wealthy San Francisco professionals and their domestic partners. The area's homes, already fabulous on their acre lots surrounded by mature landscaping and fifty year old palms, had taken on a new glow as designers transformed the Mediterranean-style homes into mini-palazzos, with topiary ducks and pools ringed with boulders trucked down from the mountains and lowered into place with huge cranes. Unfortunately for Paula, no one in the Las Palmas ever responded to her letters, and she found it impossible to knock-doors on houses surrounded by electric gates and fifteen-foot-high privacy hedges. She had called all the phone numbers listed in the tax-assessors office, most of which were out-of-service or which connected to voice mail. Lately she had taken to driving through the area handing out business cards to area gardeners, with a promise of a reward if they helped her get business. The gardeners would take the cards and listen to her politely, nodding and smiling but without comprehending a word she was saying, since most spoke only Spanish.

Still Paula persisted. She felt sure that just one big listing in the area would lead to another, then another and another in a snowball effect that would soon have Dionne Searcey on the run. If only she could get her foot in the door.

* * *

A few hours later, as she was dragging her heavy bag of agent paraphernalia to her cubicle at the Windsong office, Paula got her chance. The phone started to ring just as she approached the desk.

"Paula Cooper-Price," she answered.

"Did you get it?" demanded the crackly male voice on the other end, the papery voice of an old man.

"Did I get what?"

"Did you get the price?"

"Who is this?" Paula asked, thinking someone in the office was playing a joke on her.

"It's Bill. Bill Bulkley."

"Bill Bulkley," Paula repeated, mentally running through the short list of her elderly male acquaintances. "I'm not sure I know you."

"Sure you do," said Bulkley. "We talked last week. I'm the old coot on Oro Grande."

Suddenly it clicked. A week earlier she had been fantasy cruising through Las Palmas, looking for the Donald O'Connor honeymoon home, when a white-haired man in plastic sandals and plaid shorts had tottered out of a wooden gate to fetch the mail. Before he could disappear, Paula had run over and thrust her business card into his gnarled hands, causing him to drop his letters, which she then had to gather without letting her dress ride too far up her thighs. Her embarrassment amused the man, who smiled at her with a crooked grin, revealing his chipped, yellow teeth.

"Yes, Mr. Bulkley, I remember you now," she said. "What can I do for you?"

"What do you mean what can you do for me? You were going to let me know the price."

"What price?" said Paula, who didn't remember this part of their conversation at all.

"I thought we went over all this," the man said, sounding annoyed. "The price we could set for my house."

"Oh yes, *that* price," said Paula, a red alert going off in her brain. She plopped herself before her computer and logged into the title company web site. A little sign taped to the monitor read, "Get the appointment!"

"Not that I want to sell," said Bulkley.

"I understand," said Paula. "We'll take it one step at a time. What was that address again?"

"14 Oro Grande," Bulkley said. "It's just that Pat keeps bugging me and bugging me."

"Who's Pat?"

"How old are you?"

"Why?"

"Because your memory is worse than mine, and I'm 89."

When Paula found Bulkley's address in the database, her eyes bugged out: 6 bedrooms, 4 baths on 1.3 acres with a pool. House built in 1935, probably a hacienda, no mortgage—Bulkley had planted himself there fifty years earlier and hadn't left since. The lot alone was worth over a million; the entire estate, with a guest house, had to be worth three times that at least.

"When did you want to meet?" Paula asked.

"I don't want to meet," Bulkley said. "I just want to know what my house is worth."

"Mr. Bulkley," Paula said quickly, "If I give you a number over the phone, it just wouldn't be fair. I have to go over your property, get an idea of its physical condition, the landscaping, the amenities, know what goes with the property and what stays."

"Weren't you just over here?"

"Well, yes, but I need to see the inside."

The old man hesitated, confused. He wasn't quite as sharp as he initially sounded. "Didn't you see the inside?" he said at last.

"No, Mr. Bulkley, but it will only take a few minutes and then I can give you that value you're looking for."

More hesitation on the other side of the line.

"Oh, all right," Bulkley said. "Stop by this afternoon. I'm always here. I don't have anyplace else to go."

* * *

"I've got a listing appointment in Las Palmas!" Paula exclaimed to Krystyna Kurzydlowski, the agent from Poland who sat in the cubicle next to hers. Everyone called her K.K.

"Wow, great," said K.K., her face a pale oval framed by the huge ball of red hair. "Just make sure your presentation is top-notch. Everything's got to be really slick to make an impression over there. You know—like those things Dionne Searcey puts together."

Paula's heart sank. The "things" Dionne Searcey put together for her prospective clients were slick, oversized flip-charts of text and graphics with aluminum covers and paper made by some artist in Los Angeles. In fact, the whole thing looked more like an artist's portfolio than a sales presentation. Paula had seen one once at a Realtor Association meeting, on the table of an agent from the Team Searcey office. It weighed at least ten pounds.

Paula's own presentations were much more mundane. Windsong published a number of flyers with titles like "Marketing Your Home with Windsong" and "The Power of a Windsong Open House." Paula would collect a packet of the brochures, add a few business cards and samples of ads snipped from the paper, and slip it all into a nice glossy folder with a picture of a Victorian mansion on the cover. Her clients seemed satisfied, though the Victorian mansion always bothered Paula. There weren't any Victorian mansions in Palm Springs, which had been a plain of drifting sand when Victoria ruled the high seas.

Paula thought back to her conversation with Bulkley, trying to get a picture of him in her mind. Old, yes; rich, definitely–but folksy rich, not obnoxious rich; probably drove an ancient Plymouth. Cantankerous and used to getting his own way. His memory was a little shaky, not surprising in a man his age. Health seemed good, title in his name only though that didn't mean he wasn't married. Was his wife still alive, or did he wander around the big old house alone? Probably had some kind of live-in attendant. Maybe that was Pat.

In the copy room, she assembled her usual listing presentation and looked at it in despair. It seemed thin considering the size of the property, even when she added in the lengthy property report she had downloaded from the title company and stuffed the folder full of every Windsong flyer she could get her hands on. Then she remembered the coffee table in the lobby. It was chock full of glossy magazines like *Desert Golf* and *Prestige Homes*–real estate porn designed to plant home-buying fantasies in the minds of prospective clients. A half-dozen of these, along with the lengthy contracts and the folder she had already put together, would fit nicely into the translucent plastic file case that had been gathering dust under her desk. You could still see the Victorian mansion through the plastic, and the entire package, with the thick spring fashion issue of *Palm Springs Life* thrown in, weighed at least eleven pounds—one pound more than a Dionne Searcey presentation.

Now all she had to do was get the listing.

* * *

At the wooden gate of the estate, Paula identified herself over the intercom and was buzzed in. Inside the wall, a long, L-shaped ranch house cozied itself against a turquoise swimming pool, both set off by enormously high groves of palm trees that must have been planted in the 30s, when the house was built. The landscaping was neglected. Yellow palm fronds lay scattered around the thinning grass, and the ficus trees which lined the walls were the size of oaks and cast dense shadows over the house, which gave off an air of genteel decadence. One corner of the clay tile roof, she noted, was covered by a faded tarpaulin, and as she got near the pool she noticed that the brick decking was heaved and cracked. A fixer, she realized to her disappointment, although a multi-million dollar fixer with magnificent views of Mt. San Jacinto, which glistened white with snow beyond the forbidding ficus.

"Oh," said the woman waiting for her at the door. She was a slender blonde in tailored black pants and crisply ironed white blouse. Adorning her neck was a simple but elegant gold necklace from which hung a single enormous black pearl. She looked to be in her early forties; Paula assumed she must be Pat and that Pat must be Bulkley's daughter. "Are you with the team?"

"The team?" said Paula, taking the woman's extended hand.

"Don't you call it a team? Where are your helpers? Anyway, come in. I want to go over a few things with you before we see Bill."

Mystified, Paula followed the woman through an enormous, shuttered living room into a small but tidy kitchen in the back of the house. The kitchen was of burgundy tile, with white-painted wooden cabinets and molding scalloped at the edges, probably last remodeled shortly after Pearl Harbor. She led Paula to a tiny table looking out through a screened door to the back wall of the house—the service entrance.

"Have a seat," the woman said. "I was just making some tea."

She turned her back to Paula, who sat at a table covered in a red-and-white checked vinyl tablecloth. On the chair to her right was a sight that explained everything: one of Dionne Searcey's aluminum-covered presentations. Numbly, Paula picked it up, turning the heavy cream pages until she came to a line drawing of the house which looked as if it had been etched by Rembrandt.

Abruptly, Paula closed the book, feeling ill. Clearly, somehow, the woman thought that she was with Dionne Searcey, and clearly, somehow, Paula was going to have to disabuse her of that notion, incur Bill Bulkley's wrath, and sew yet another slip cover for her cat-battered sofa. She was about to open her mouth to make just such a revelation when the woman, who was standing over the kettle waiting for it to whistle, began to speak.

"Dionne probably told you that Bill, well, he's a little reluctant to sell, but I've been working on him, and, as long as we can get the price, I don't think we'll have a problem. I assume you have all the papers ready, so you just leave everything to me as far as getting his signature. You don't have a problem with that, I'm sure. I told Dionne and I'm telling you, he's a little off and so might get cantankerous, but don't worry. He can be emotional, but of course he doesn't always know what's best. So long as we're agreed on that, I don't have any problem with Dionne's 8% commission, and we'll get the repairs and landscaping done as we discussed." The woman turned and placed at the table two mis-matched mugs of tea, the bags floating on the top. "Here you go," she said. "There's milk on the counter–I'm sorry, I just realized I don't know your name."

"Paula," Paula said. "Paula Cooper-Price."

Now of course was the opportunity to explain the terrible mix-up as to her identity, but before she could launch into an explanation the woman took a seat across from her and started talking again.

"The big thing," the woman said, "is the price. I know it's not in top shape but we need to get as much as we can for the place, considering our time-line. I've gone over the comps you gave me and I really think three-point-four is what we want to go with, unless Dionne found out anything terribly different."

"No," said Paula, rigidly erect. "$3.4 million is a good price."

"Fine," said the woman. "We better go over the listing papers before we see him and mark where he's supposed to sign. His eyesight's not so good."

Slowly, heart pounding, Paula undid the string on her plastic presentation folder, knowing that stealing Dionne Searcey's listing was wrong, both from the standpoint of the Realtor Code of Ethics and from the standpoint of Judeo-Christian morality and the wrath of a just God, but she was unable to suppress the rising surge of the excitement she felt at beating Dionne Searcey at her own game, and in just the way Searcey had beaten her. After all, her grandmother used to say, all's fair in love and war.

Of course, her grandmother also used to say two wrongs do not make a right, but Paula pushed that out of her mind as she penned in a purchase price of $3.4 million and a commission of 8.0% on the Exclusive

Residential Listing Agreement. Eight percent, that was something like $300,000 in commission, split of course with whoever brought in the buyer, unless she could double-end the deal. But no, better not to get greedy, better to assume someone else brought in the buyer, she'd still make half that–enough to live on for three years, or two years if she went crazy at Panache Interiors.

Automatically, as she had done a hundred times before, she started explaining the agreement paragraph-by-paragraph, carefully covering the name "Windsong" with her thumb, but after a few moments the woman stopped her.

"I'm sure that's all standard. Just show me where he signs," said the woman.

"Well, we have lots of different documents, but these are the important ones to get us started. We need his initials here and here and his signature here and here."

"Fine," said the woman, taking the documents. "Leave everything to me."

Paula watched as the woman made enormous Xs with a black marker beside the signature lines, feeling guilty because everything was going so smoothly that she had nothing to do. "Do you live here with your father?" Paula said, just to be making some noise.

"My father?" the woman said, puzzled. Then she laughed. "I forgot we hadn't met before. I'm Pat Anka. Bill is my boyfriend."

* * *

At Six Flags Magic Mountain the previous summer, Paula's son Michael had coaxed her into riding the Super Cobra roller coaster, calming her fears by pointing out that all the people who were getting on were also getting off. But the minute the train started jerking up the first hill, topping the trees and rising higher and higher until the trucks on the adjacent freeway looked like tiny toys, Paula knew she had made a mistake. Beyond that first hill, the track dipped and twisted like a skein of tangled yarn, and Paula was along for the ride, powerless to affect her trajectory.

She felt like that now, as she went with the woman to find Bill Bulkley, fighting back the impulse to snatch back the listing agreement and flee. The nature of the relationship between Ms. Anka and Mr. Bulkley was none of her business, she told herself. Perhaps Ms. Anka was just a take-charge kind of woman. Who was Paula to say true love couldn't exist between a woman-of-a-certain age and a man a half-century her senior? And who could put a price on the comfort and companionship a pretty woman like Pat Anka could offer an elderly man all by himself in the world? In fact, there was even a real estate concept, "love and affection," that could be used to value a gift of real property in the state of California. Money was just money, but love and affection was priceless. Perhaps Bulkley had an excess of the former and a dearth of the latter.

Paula was there not to judge but to facilitate, she decided. As they entered the dark, overheated room where Bill Bulkley sat in his stocking feet watching *Oprah*, she vowed to keep her mouth shut whatever happened. No more shooting herself in the foot. She had a child to feed and furniture to buy. If Dionne Searcey could take the heat, she could too.

"Hello, daddy," said Pat Anka, greeting Bill Bulkley with a kiss on his age-spotted forehead. His hair was white and thin but there was still plenty of it on his head. "This is Paula. She's a real estate agent from Dionne Searcey's team."

He squinted at her fiercely. "I know you," he said, and for a moment Paula thought he was about to denounce her for the fraud she was. But then he concluded: "You're the one who made me drop the mail."

"That's right," said Paula. "We met on the street," she explained to Pat, quickly, to move the conversation on.

"And now you're here to cheat me out of my house," said Bulkley, not bitterly but matter-of-factly.

"That's not very nice," said Pat, taking a seat on the couch and curling up her long legs so that the soft fabric of her tailored pants pressed against the old man's skinny thighs. "Paula's here to help us."

"Help rob me, you mean," the old man said, in the same tone. "She thinks because I'm old I don't know the score," he said to Paula, who took a seat across from him and kept a tight-lipped smile pasted on her face.

"Now, dad, that will be enough of that," Pat said. "We talked about this a million times."

"She wants me to sell so we can move to Florida," Bill Bulkley said to Paula. "Ever been to Florida? Nothing but manatees and mosquitoes."

"We have a nice condo picked out in South Beach," the woman explained to Paula. "I need to get him somewhere where there's a little life around."

"There's life around here," said Bill Bulkley. "I don't hear you complaining about life at bed time." To Paula's surprise Pat Anka blushed, and Bulkley winked at Paula, grinning furiously. Paula kept the smile in place, but was taken aback. Bulkley seemed pretty sharp, but at his age could the acuity of his mental parts possibly be matched by the acuity of other parts which demanded periodic servicing?

"Now daddy, Paula's brought the papers and I don't want any argument from you about signing them.." She took the contracts and smoothed them out on his lap, using a big coffee table book as a writing surface.

Bulkley pushed them away, irritated.

"I told you I'm still thinking," he said.

"Don't let's start that again," the woman said. "I'm not staying in this old house another minute."

"What's wrong with it? I like it here."

"You'll like it more in Florida," she said.

"I was stationed at the Marine Flying Field during the war you know," the old man told Paula.

"Yes, dad, we know," said Pat. "But can we keep focused here for a minute?" She put the papers back in Bulkley's lap and handed him a pen. "You said if we could get three-point-four we'd sell. Well, Paula's going to get us three-point-four. Isn't that right, Paula?"

"That's right," said Paula, the smile still on her face.

"Three-point-four million," Bill Bulkley said, squinting at the contract. "That's a lot of money."

"And we'll still have a lot left over after we pay for the condo," Pat Anka pointed out.

"You'll have a lot left over, you mean. I'll be dead."

"Nobody's going to die anytime soon," said the woman.

"I will. I don't know a single soul in Miami."

"You'll make friends," said Pat. "They got that senior citizen center right by the beach."

"Old coots," said Bill Bulkley.

"You'll have me," the woman said.

"I have you here."

Pat stiffened. "I've been good to you, haven't I, dad?"

"Yes, you've been good to me."

"Then let's get out of this old place and have some fun. You promised."

"I promised I'd think about it."

"Come on, you're making Paula wait," said the woman. "I'll help you."

She took Bulkley's hand in hers and attempted to guide his pen to the paper. He resisted, resulting in a scrawl where his signature was supposed to go.

"God damn you, woman," said Bulkley.

Pat Anka sat upright and clamped her hand around Bulkley's wasted bicep. "Pick up that pen," she commanded.

"You can keep your Florida," he said defiantly.

"Pick it up," she warned, squeezing harder.

Bulkley squirmed under her grip. "You're hurting me," he said.

Paula was about to break them apart when Pat let go. "Alright," the woman said, her eyes hard. "Stay here if you want. But if you don't sign those papers get someone else to soak your dentures and change your sheets." She turned to Paula. "He thinks he's a stud but I have to mix his Viagra with applesauce."

Bill Bulkley shrank back at this cruelty, seeming to sink into the fabric of the couch. "But I like Palm Springs," he said in a weak, little-boy voice.

"I've had enough of your nonsense. I'm going to South Beach with or without you."

Bulkley's resolution went out of him like a pricked balloon. He picked up the pen and pulled the documents to his lap. "It's not right," he said.

"You promised," Pat said.

He shook his head in disgust but began signing, not bothering to read the text. Pat squealed, sat down again with her thighs against his, and took the papers from him one by one.

"There," Bulkley said when he was finished. "I hope you're happy."

Pat threw her arms around him and kissed him square on the mouth.

"Thanks, dad."

* * *

Paula felt grubby and depressed as she drove back to the office with the multi-million dollar contract in her bag, the warm afternoon sunlight pouring into her lap. She tried to steer her mind toward how she would market the house (glossy ads in *Distinctive Homes*, a TV spot on "Desert Real Estate," an exclusive open house/cocktail party for all the heavy-hitter agents in town), but what she kept seeing in her mind's eye was Pat Anka's bejeweled hand tightened like a hose clamp around Bill Bulkley's pathetic biceps.

The thing was, her grandfather had had arms like that when her Grandma Ruth was taking care of him. He was dying of stomach cancer, and when Paula and her mother would come to visit, Grandma would help him from his bed to a chair near the window, her hand wrapped around his arm. Paula, who was then seven, was agog at the skeletal thinness of that arm, which even then she knew presaged something terrible.

At the stop light on East Palm Canyon, Paula turned on the radio and began punching the buttons furiously, looking for some upbeat music to drive the negativity from her mind. A Top Producer agent had to be positive at all times, the sales coach she had briefly hired had told her. Happy people got happy results. Beautiful work for beautiful pay. When a negative thought entered your mind, push the pause button and say to yourself, "erase, erase, erase."

"Erase, erase, erase," Paula said to herself, aloud, in the idling car. "Erase, erase, erase." She was a top-selling agent with multiple high-end listings. Her positive mental attitude attracted enthusiastic, wealthy customers. She opened the gate to the Golden Road to Riches by turning the Silver Key of Willingness.

Skinny arm.

Damn.

* * *

"You want me to do *what?*" said Lee Kidwell, the broker-manager back at the Windsong office.

"You heard me," said Paula, who had closed the door to Kidwell's office behind her so that the other neb-nose agents wouldn't get wind of what was going on.

"I don't know," said Kidwell, running his hand through his hair. "We're talking about a huge commission here. You've got a signed contract."

"Signed under duress," said Paula.

"Duress says you. You're not an attorney," Kidwell countered. He was trying to weigh the need for legal caution against the company's interest in making money. The contract wasn't official until he signed off on it as the brokerage company's representative. Paula found herself in the awkward position of trying to convince Kidwell that he should disapprove the signed listing agreement she had just brought him.

"She brow beat him. No way he would have signed it otherwise."

"Did she hold a gun to his head? Because if she didn't I'm inclined to save you from yourself here," said Kidwell.

"It stinks, Lee. She's stealing the house out from under him."

"Are you saying he's not competent?"

"Well, no, but..."

"I don't get you, Paula. This is your best contract ever and you want to let it go." He leaned back in his chair and peered at her through steepled hands. "I think you're just afraid of success. I'm going to initial this."

"That's not such a good idea," said Paula, squirming. "There's something else."

Just then the phone rang. Kidwell picked it up. A voice on the other end began talking rapidly, and Kidwell looked at Paula sharply. He listened for a long time and said, "All right, she's in my office right now. I'll investigate and get back to you."

He hung and turned to Paula. "Did you impersonate Dionne Searcey to get this listing?"

"Ah, not exactly," said Paula.

"Her lawyer says you did. Her lawyer says you presented yourself under false pretenses and stole a listing Searcey had already wrapped up."

"She didn't have it wrapped up," Paula said, annoyed at the imputation of her salesmanship skills. "And I never claimed to be Dionne Searcey."

"'You never *claimed*,'" Kidwell said. "Did they think you were her or not?"

"Well, that was the other thing I was about to tell you," said Paula. "They might have been, ah, under the impression I was working with her, yes."

He ran his hand through his thinning hair. "I should have known it would be something like this."

"What do you mean?"

"All this bullshit about duress and fraud and incompetence–when did you figure out Dionne Searcey was going to sue your ass? On the way back to the office?"

"That never even occurred to me," Paula said.

"Don't give me that crap," said Kidwell. "You thought you'd get revenge for the Faircloughs by stealing Searcey's big listing, then got cold feet."

He tossed the contract across the desk to Paula. "Here, you got your wish, there's no way Windsong's getting involved with this. Take it and get out."

Red-faced, Paula picked up the contract and rose.

Kidwell rubbed his forehead. "This is really a screw up, Paula. You'll be lucky to keep your license if she goes after you. What do you want to mess with Dionne Searcey for?"

* * *

That evening, Paula sat numbly before the TV, spooning into her mouth the last of a pint of Rocky Road ice cream that she had sworn she would just have a bite of. She already felt fat. Her son, Michael, was still at wrestling practice and Larry, her on-again-off-again boyfriend, was up in Las Vegas on some rights-management issue. The Comedy Channel skit depicted the President as a baby who persisted in dirtying his diapers while being tried in Kyoto for environmental crimes. The smell was so bad that Ted Kennedy, his lawyer, abandoned his defense and Al Gore, his judge, was driven from the court before he could pronounce sentence. That must have been the end of the skit because the studio audience was shown applauding wildly before a commercial came on for a Toyota pickup. "With an available 381-horsepower 5.7-liter V8 engine, the new Tundra is no ordinary half-ton," the ad proclaimed.

She clicked off the remote and stood, then realized she had nowhere to go and sat down again. She was a fool and an idiot. $300,000 was a lot of money to let slip through her fingers over some quaint mid-western qualm about conniving young women in slacks. She imagined what it would be like if the Comedy Channel got wind of the episode. She would be the hayseed farmer's daughter, barefoot and pregnant, trading away the family's valuable antiques for a jewel-encrusted bible that, it turned out, had too many big words in it for her to actually read.

No. She had had a signed contract and if Dionne Searcey didn't like it Paula could have told her to take a hike, jump in a lake, stick her thumb up her ass. In fact, those were the exact words she should have used: "Dionne, jump in a lake, and while you're at it go stick a thumb up your ass." What, after all, could Searcey have done? Sue Paula and reveal to all the world her little money grubbing conspiracy to steal the old man's house?

Paula hated Dionne Searcey, and there was only one thing she could think to do about it: slash the tires of Dionne Searcey's Lexus, the way she had once slashed the tires of Amy Freret' father's Lincoln when Amy Freret had called her flat and got her dis-invited to the high school junior prom that she really didn't want to go to anyway.

She rose from the couch to look for a suitable knife.

* * *

Locating Dionne's car was more difficult than she thought, but she finally hit pay dirt at Brush, the former ranchette of Trini Lopez, now a trendy restaurant much favored by the real estate *glitterati*. Brush was a complex of stucco-ed buildings circling a lantern-illuminated court yard. Paula parked on an adjacent street and from the shadows examined the crowded tables one-by-one until she spotted Dionne Searcey, quaffing an appletini and laughing giddily with Pat Anka, who was picking at a salad. Sitting silently in front of a steak the size of Rhode Island was Bill Bulkley, trussed in an ill-fitting suit with a necktie so tight folds of skin drooped over the pointed white collar. He was staring at his plate through a pair of black reading glasses, as if it were a poem to be parsed.

Paula made her way to the parking lot in the rear, entering in a gap between two dusty oleanders. The knife—one of a cheap set she had picked up at the Cabazon Outlets—was concealed in the pocket of her Realtor bag. If anyone saw her coming or going, she could pretend she was meeting a client for dinner.

Dionne's Lexus GS was the second car down from the dumpster, and as soon as the monkey-jacketed parking valet finished retrieving a yellow Hummer for some waiting patron out front, Paula boldly crossed the lot. A quick glance in the Lexus' back seat revealed several Dionne Searcey brochures—confirming that Paula had the right car—and, on the passenger side, a monstrous cellophane-wrapped gift basket, probably a present for Searcey's new "clients." The sight of the gift basket, with its individually wrapped pears and be-ribboned tins of imported chocolates, had to cost at least $300, a sum Paula found cynically small compared to the commission Searcey was fleecing from her victims.

The lot was deserted. Paula stooped down between Searcey's car and the adjacent Scion and fumbled in the dark for the knife. A small pool of antifreeze formed a puddle near the front tire, and Paula carefully stepped around it. The Lexus had oversized mag wheels, arranged like wagon spokes around a central hub, and tires with fashionably narrow sidewalls only half the width of a conventional tire.

Perhaps because of the narrowness of the sidewall, Paula's first stab missed, the knife blade burying itself ineffectually in the tire's tread. Her second stab was better, but when she pulled out the blade, not only could she not hear the expected hiss, she couldn't even locate the entry wound.

She tried again, this time carefully bracing herself against the fender to get better leverage. The knife sank in much deeper this time, at least a half inch, and Paula wiggled the blade up and down and right and left in an attempt to enlarge the hole, breaking off the plastic handle in the process.

Paula was puzzled. It had taken no such effort to ruin the tires of Amy Freret's dad's car. In fact, she had been able to do the deed with a fairly dull pen knife she had stolen from her grandfather's tool box, all four tires, *phiff!*, one after another in Buckeye High parking lot. Had sidewall technology improved that much since her wayward youth, or did Searcey's car sport some kind of primo puncture proof Japanese uber-tire?

She was pondering these complexities and trying to work the knife out of the tire when she heard footsteps across the lot and looked up to see Dionne Searcey heading straight for the car. Paula abandoned her attempt to withdraw the knife blade and instead scooted around to the passenger side of the vehicle, keeping below the hood line so as not to be spotted. Searcey was digging in her purse for her keys. Only when she clicked the automatic door locks did Paula realize Searcey was heading not for the driver's door but straight for her, on the passenger side; she was evidently coming to retrieve the gift basket.

Paula was trapped. She felt a quick panic as she looked for some way, any way, to crawl or climb or run away from the jam she had gotten herself in, but she was blocked in by the dumpster on one side and the approaching Dionne on the other. Maybe, she reflected, selling high-end real estate wasn't the niche market she should be concentrating on. Yes, she hated her sofa, but perhaps her perception of the damage done by the cats was exaggerated, something she could cure with a nice slip cover from Stein Mart instead of a big Las Palmas listing and a year in jail. The worst of it was, she had left her Realtor bag with her Department of Real Estate I.D. lying by Searcey's drivers side tire, right beside the knife.

Searcey was only yards away now. Paula steeled herself and began to rise. The only thing she could think of was to make a headlong run past Searcey and out of the lot; maybe some miracle would save her.

Just then, a Bach fugue began to play, but a Bach fugue as it would sound in hell, a distorted, electronic, soulless, square electronic *booping* that turned out to be Dionne Searcey's cell ring tone. Searcey paused a few yards from her car and frantically began trying to fish the phone out of her purse, turning slightly toward a distant street light and retrieving the device just as the ringing stopped. She stared near-sightedly at the glowing number and put the phone back into her purse.

The cell phone gave Paula an idea. When Dionne Searcey turned, she found Paula casually propped against the hood of the adjacent car, a hand cupped to her face.

"Of course we can meet at the property," she was saying. "Yes, ten a.m., that would be good. See you then." With her back still to Searcey, she made a gesture as if flipping shut the imaginary phone and twisted around to "see" Searcey for the first time.

"Oh, hello," Paula said.

"You startled me," said Dionne Searcey. "I didn't see you there." She was sheathed in a tight dark green dress that contrasted perfectly with her smooth pale shoulders.

Paula braced herself and said nothing. Searcey stepped forward and peered at Paula in the darkness. Paula peered back at her, her face a neutral mask.

"You're that Cooper woman," Searcey said with a gasp.

"And you're that Searcey woman."

"What are you doing here?" she demanded.

"This is my car," said Paula, patting the hood of the burgundy Scion where she was perched. "I was talking to a client."

Dionne shot her a contemptuous glance. "Bullshit," she said. "What do you want?"

"That gift basket."

"What?"

"I want the gift basket." Paula had had no intention of asking for the basket or anything else. All she had wanted was to get away. But Searcey's superior attitude galled her.

"You're crazy. That's for my clients."

Paula snorted. "Aren't you ashamed of yourself? Stealing that house out from that old man?"

"You are out of your mind," Searcey said. "I'm not stealing anything."

"Right," said Paula.

"Everything I have I've worked for," Searcey said bitterly. "Not that it's any of your business. I could have your license for what you pulled today."

"I could have yours," Paula said.

It was the simple truth. Searcey seemed shocked by the idea and searched Paula's face to see if she was bluffing. Finally, she took a step back.

"Look, if I give you the basket will you go away?"

"For now," said Paula.

"What's that mean?"

"I'm farming Las Palmas and I'm not going to stop."

"Fine," said Searcey.

Searcey opened the passenger door and handed Paula the gift basket.

"You're not getting any money you know."

"I don't want your money," said Paula, hefting the basket in her hands. It weighed about 30 pounds and smelled faintly of vanilla and cinnamon.

"Anything else?" said Searcey.

"Just let me get my knife," said Paula. "It's sticking in your front tire."

Paula walked around to the driver's side and wiggled the knife free from the tire, which still refused to deflate.

Dionne Searcey blanched and stepped back. "You're crazy," she said. "You're really crazy."

Paula scooped the gift basket from the hood and brushed by Searcey, walking briskly toward the gap in the oleanders. I *am* crazy, she thought. But at least I'm not Dionne Searcey.

She couldn't wait to get home to open her gift basket. It was such a nice gesture. You had to hand it to Dionne. She had class.

———◆———

[YOU'RE FADING OUT]

Paula Cooper-Price had been trying to reach Chucky Milo off and on for the better part of two days when she finally heard the call connecting. She immediately pulled the Rover to the side of the road, prompting a horn-burst from the blue Aveo that had been riding her tail.

Clamping her hand over her free ear, she listened intently to the faint international ringing on the other end of the line—a feeble, broken sound like the bleating of a dying goat. Finally there was a barely perceptible voice:

"Hello?"

"Hello, Chucky?" Paula said.

"Hello? Hello?"

"Chucky, it's Paula from Windsong," she said, exaggerating the enunciation of each word as if talking to a hearing-impaired child. "Can you hear me? I need to talk to you. Hello?"

There was a *click* as the connection broke and Paula sighed. She immediately punched the redial button but all she heard were faint whines and computer bloops as the call once again hung in cyberspace.

Her client, the Internet mogul Chucky Milo, was on a yacht somewhere in the Indonesian peninsula and she needed to talk to him about a problem with the BIA lease. All Realtors relied on their faxes, their cell phones, their multiple email accounts, their laptops, desktops, Blackberries and Treos and Palm Pilots to keep in touch with distant clients, but sometimes Paula felt like all that technology made it harder to actually connect with a real person. She sighed and dropped the phone into the Rover's cup holder; maybe she could reach Milo on the land line from the office.

* * *

The office was eerily deserted.

"Where is everyone?" she asked Lureen, the smooth-complexioned music student who was Windsong Palm Springs' receptionist.

"Let's see, Lee is meeting with Ruth in Indian Wells, Kyle is in San Diego for that ADA thing, and Lummy had to run to the uptown office to meet the fire inspector. I don't know where all the agents are. K.K. is back there, I think."

But K.K., Paula's cube mate, wasn't back there. A message on Paula's computer screen reminded her that Herm Horvat's birthday was in three days. She didn't know who Herm Horvat was, so she clicked the "dismiss" button, revealing another message that said "call Chucky Milo."

"I'm trying," she said to the computer. Milo, on the other side of the International Date Line, was 3 hours and 1 day ahead of her, making it 7 a.m. Saturday in Jakarta. She picked up the desk phone and dialed Chucky's satellite number.

She got a busy signal, but given their difficulty connecting, Paula actually found that encouraging and dialed again. The line was still busy. She put the phone in speaker mode, punching the redial button mechanically as she opened her email program to scan for messages from her client. Lots of mail looking for open house help or announcing new listings, but nothing in Outlook from Milo, and nothing on her Hotmail, Yahoo, Gmail, or AOL accounts either.

Milo was, of course, the former hacker who—with his fellow former hacker Tip Midon—had made a fortune selling software to protect big corporate servers from hackers like themselves. They famously called their company "Chucky and Tip" and took turns running it six months at a time. Chucky was on month three of his six months off. He was 24.

Paula knew squat about the Internet, but she knew enough about who Chucky Milo was to give him her full attention when he had wandered into her open house at the Elrod-designed mid-century condo at the Racquet Club three weeks earlier. Dressed in a baggy "Do No Thing" sweatshirt and accompanied by a gaggle of giggling friends not much older than Paula's son, Milo had looked around, taken her card, and called her back thirty minutes later to say he'd take it, all cash, providing she could negotiate an acceptable price with the sellers and do all the paperwork by fax and Internet and satellite phone since he was already on the plane to a conference in Davos, Switzerland.

This unusual arrangement, when accompanied by the name "Chucky Milo," actually resulted in a swift deal, and Paula was feeling pretty proud of herself until the seller, an anal-retentive lawyer from L.A., had balked at paying for a renewal on the Bureau of Indian Affairs land lease underlying the property. (Half of Palm Springs was built on land owned by the Cahuilla Indians, who leased their land for long intervals to homeowners.)

The lawyer's intransigence threatened to unravel all of Paula's hard work, and she couldn't resolve the problem until she talked to her client, who by now had abandoned snowy Switzerland for his cruise somewhere in the South China sea—one of those exclusive rich-people no-set-itinerary wind-jammin' things in a restored Chinese junk.

For a moment, one of her redial attempts seemed poised to connect, as she again heard the computer beeps and dying goat noises. Then a tired mechanical voice announced, "I'm sorry. All circuits are busy now. Please try your call later."

Paula decided to give up for now. Chucky Milo would have to wait.

* * *

Paula arrived home with a trunk full of groceries to find her 14 year old son, Michael, furiously stuffing clothes into his new $90 sports bag.

"Mom," he yelled, the moment she poked her head in the door. "Where have you been? I'm going to be late."

"I forgot, honey," said Paula. With all the stress of dealing with Chucky Milo, she had forgotten that Michael was going camping with the Marine youth group. She was supposed to have him at the church parking lot by 5 p.m. Between his raging hormones and his inability to make friends at the new school, her son had been especially hard to deal with lately and the last thing she wanted was another fight. "You should have called," she offered lamely.

"I texted, like, a dozen times."

"Your mother was busy," Paula said.

"You're always busy," he said.

The truth was, she dreaded checking text messages ever since she had started getting bombarded with text ads for a gay chat service. Michael said that the reason he left text messages for her instead of calling is that whenever he called all she did was drill him. To her mind, all she was did was express a little normal parental concern about where he was and what he was doing. Not that she was ever able to get a straight answer out of him about things like that. Lately it seemed that everything he told her was a lie, and she had secretly checked with the school to make sure there really was a Marine youth group and that it really was going camping at Big Bear.

"Do you have everything?" she asked as he zipped the bag.

"Yes I have everything," Michael said sarcastically. "I'm not a baby. Sergeant Mayfield gave us a list."

"Then let's go, Marine," Paula said, opening the door so that Michael could drag his bulging bag out to the driveway.

"If I miss the bus it's your fault," Michael said.

The remark made Paula feel inexplicably sad, and the rest of the ride to the church was glum and silent. She didn't know how to talk to Michael anymore. If she took an interest in what he was doing, like when he started to build a surfboard in the garage (his friend Derek went surfing at Laguna), he accused her of interfering in his plans and simultaneously not being helpful enough in obtaining tools and materials. If she ignored his gross manners and noisy demands, he would stomp off to sulk in his messy room, plugging his ears into his iPod and covering his head with a pillow. (At least she didn't have to listen to the thrashing rock music he liked to play; she had moved the computer and speakers out of his bedroom after she found a folder marked "bgirls" that was full of raunchy porn.) He had even gotten into trouble with the cops, rounded up at some keg party in a canyon in Desert Hot Springs. He claimed he was just "hanging," but a discreet whiff revealed breath that smelled like beer and Altoids. He didn't seem drunk, however, so she let that one pass.

"What are you going to do at camp?" Paula asked as they neared the church.

"What do you care? You're not going."

She let that pass, too. "Will there be singing around the campfire? We used to do that when I was in Girl Scouts."

"This isn't *Girl Scouts*, Mom, this is the *Marines*, he said. Then, after a minute: "We're learning rock climbing if you have to know."

She turned left on Racquet Club, and then into the church parking lot, where a grungy group of kids were hanging around a malevolent looking military truck tricked out in desert camouflage colors. A fat guy in fatigues was opening the truck's tail gate.

"Is that Sergeant Mayfield?" Paula asked, wondering if she should give him her number in case of emergency.

Michael gave her a look like she was an idiot and pointed to a spot near the church door, away from the truck. "I'll get out there," he said. He was out in a flash, dragging the heavy bag behind him.

"Have a nice time," Paula called after him.

Her son didn't even look back.

* * *

Just as she was trying to wedge her car between the walls of junk that cluttered her garage, the cell phone rang. She picked it up.

"Hello, Paula? It's Chucky Milo. Can you hear me now?"

Paula, still maneuvering into the tight space, stopped and threw the car into park. "Perfectly," she said. The connection was loud and clear, with only a faint delay as their voices bounced back and forth among the satellites far out in space. "I've been trying to reach you since Wednesday," she said.

"The weather's been crazy here," Milo said. "We had a squall blowing in the Makassar Strait all this week but it's clear now. We're anchored off Surabaya. Nora's just putting on her snorkeling gear." Nora was her client's girlfriend of the moment, a tall dark super-model Milo had met in Moscow.

"Sounds like fun," Paula said. She never knew how much chit-chat was appropriate before getting down to business. "I snorkeled once in Lake Erie."

"Oh, Erie," said Milo. "That's in Limerick, right? I stayed at a castle there with Steve Jobs."

It didn't seem worth explaining the that Lake Erie, U.S.A. was nowhere near Limerick, Ireland, so Paula lurched into the topic at hand.

"Anyway, I was calling about the Elrod condo," she said.

"Hold on a minute," Milo said. She heard some commotion on the other end of the line and Milo shouting something about an anchor line. Then he was back.

"Sorry. Nora was having trouble with her mask. We're going night fishing on the reef. Where were we?"

"The condo," Paula reminded him. "The seller's raising a stink about the lease."

"Didn't catch that."

"I said, the seller's raising a stink about the lease. He doesn't want to pay the renewal fee."

"Must be switching satellites... The connection's breaking up a bit."

"The seller's giving us trouble on the lease renewal."

"All I caught is something about fleas."

"Not fleas," Paula said into the phone, "the lease. The seller doesn't want to renew the lease."

"...fading out."

"The lease!"

"...damned antenna... lithium-ion... near the reef... tomorrow..."

"Hello? Hello?"

"Paula, you're fading out."

Once more, the connection broke.

Paula swore. She remembered reading about a spider that would store up future food by carefully wrapping its struggling prey in strand after strand of spider silk, until it was encased in a perfect little cocoon, sealed off from the world of mobility and action. She felt like that now, struggling helplessly against an invisible weave of Secure Socket Layers and peer-to-peer networks, tiny circuits working on quantum principles and satellites traveling higher and faster than any Greek god. What did she know about VPNs or ODBCs or DVIs? She was, in essence, living in a world of magic. The magicians had promised instant communications to any person anywhere in the world. They delivered, however, a smothering cocoon.

Screw it, she thought, pulling the car into the garage and unlocking the door to the kitchen, where she began fixing a salad.

Somewhere she had the name of Chucky Milo's personal attorney. She'd go into the office tomorrow and compose a letter to him, then have it hand delivered to his Silicon Valley address by overnight mail. It should be there Monday and then it would be the lawyer's problem to contact Milo, not Paula's.

If only she could solve the problem of Michael's behavior as easily. She wasn't really thrilled with his involvement in the Marine youth group, since she knew the next step was high school ROTC, and then, when he was old enough, the real-life Marine Corps. She tolerated his choice, however, because A) she didn't want to fight about it, B) the Marine kids seemed preferable as companions to the stoner kids Michael otherwise hung out with, and C), Michael seemed to need some masculine influence in his life now that he only saw his father on alternate weekends; maybe Sgt. Mayfield could fill the gap?

Oh, and D), she blamed herself for making a mess of her son's life. Michael had been an active and out-going boy until the divorce trouble started, and even after the separation was heavily involved in Little League and Boy

Scouts. Since the move to Palm Springs, however, his grades had dropped off a cliff and he had become so sullen and rebellious that even her ex-husband Dale noticed, although he attributed the change in their son's personality to "teenage hormones."

The guidance counselor at the high school had a more ominous theory and had given her a pamphlet, "Is Your Child on Drugs?" It listed 10 warning signs to watch for, including No. 1, withdrawing from family, No. 4, disrespectful attitude above and beyond the norm, No. 7, slipping grades, and No. 9, disinterest in activities formerly enjoyed. The counselor suggested Paula search Michael's room for contraband and spring on him a surprise drug test, which could be analyzed by a lab in L.A. for the presence of THC, cocaine, methamphetamines and the club drug Ecstasy. "A lot of kids are doing Ecstasy," the counselor noted. She even gave Paula a container to take the urine sample in, warning her to make sure the sample was taken in her presence "so your son can't fake the results."

Paula was at first appalled by the suggestion that Michael was a drug abuser, but lately had begun to wonder, especially after the beer keg incident. Dale, of course, thought Paula's suspicions were totally off base and would have nothing to do with drug testing their son, arguing that it would destroy whatever little respect he had for them, and Paula was inclined to agree.

Her salad ready, she put the whole subject out of her mind and sat at the table to catch up on her *Realtor Magazine*, which had a cover article "Think Like a Billionaire." "Be persistent and relentless," the article extolled. "Billionaires don't let obstacles or pitfalls stand in their way; they move over, around and through the obstacles to obtain their goals." Chucky Milo was listed as a billionaire who refused to give up. Another part of the article advised getting an advanced college degree: "20 of the top 26 real estate billionaires have a college degree or higher. Only one is a high-school dropout."

Projecting ten years into the future, she thought about Michael as a former Marine sniper, now employed as Assistant Manager of the Del Taco off the Monterey Avenue I-10 exit. Then, finishing the salad, she made a beeline for her son's room. If there were drugs in there, she was going to find them.

On the surface, it was the room of a typical teenage boy, clothes dropped on the floor, posters of Randy Moss catching a football and some bizarre rock group named Slipknot pinned to the wall. A pile of *Sports Illustrated* and *Rolling Stone* magazines sat on the end table to the right of the twin bed, which Paula realized was sagging and needed replacing. A cheap desk from K-Mart sat in front of the window which faced the side yard; the closet, with its mirrored doors, was opposite the bed.

Paula hesitated in the doorway, not only uncertain about where she should begin but reluctant to undertake the search at all. To do so would be an explicit admission that she no longer trusted her son. Michael, she knew, held his privacy in high regard, and if he found out she had searched his room, he would be devastated. On the other hand, he was only 14. If he were doing drugs, she had a duty to protect him, even if it meant making him angry.

She moved to the desk and opened the drawer. Inside was a jumble of pens, paper clips, football cards, a stapler, a wad of string, a

Tic Tac candy dispenser. She opened the Tic Tac dispenser and confirmed that it contained Tic Tacs. The pencil sharpener contained pencil shavings and the Wite-Out smelled like Wite-Out, not Ecstasy or God-knows-what.

The second drawer was more of the same, but with an electronic theme. There was a USB cable, a digital camera, three rechargeable batteries, his pre-iPod MP3 player, a Street Fighter 2 video game, and a suspicious looking aluminum tube that proved to contain a Montecristo cigar. If Michael smoked cigars, that was news to her. She screwed the container back together and put it where she found it. The digital camera had shots of some kids at the street fair.

Under the bed she found a box containing old high school notebooks and, hidden under that, two *Hustler* magazines, undoubtedly stolen from his father's porn collection, which had been one of many points of contention between Paula and Dale. After the "bgirls" incident Paula had resigned herself to Michael's male sexuality so she didn't bother to get upset over the porn. The only other thing under the bed was Michael's baseball mitt and the dusty snowboard which he had immediately outgrown.

In the drawer of the nightstand she found a softbound comic book featuring a dark-haired boy with Japanese features and, tucked into that, $183 in assorted bills. This gave her pause. So far as Paula knew, Michael's only source of income was a $15 per week allowance supplied by her and Dale; was he selling drugs as well as taking them, or was he just a smart saver, a billionaire in the offing? The evidence was inconclusive. She closed the book and moved on to the closet.

Here the task seemed overwhelming. Not only was the closet stuffed full of clothes, but it was a repository for every toy, video game, CD, comic book, and piece of sports gear Michael had ever owned. She started by going through the pockets of his jeans and shirts, then decided he wouldn't be stupid enough to hide his stash where she would find it while doing laundry. She moved on to the junk on the shelf above the clothes, retrieving the step-stool from the kitchen so she could reach the board games and boxes of old photo albums and karate trophies.

All she managed to do was stir up a bunch of dust.

Relentless and determined to be thorough (a billionaire trait? she wondered), she next turned her attention to the closet floor, opening the ski goggle case, searching the pockets of his gym bag, sticking her fingers into each of the side pouches of his back pack to make sure they weren't stuffed with contraband. Nothing, not even a pack of cigarettes, not even a little locked diary like the one to which she confided her innermost thoughts when she was her son's age. Either her son was clean or he was far more clever than she ever could have been.

She had just about finished putting everything back into place when she noticed the odd shoe thrown into the closet corner. This in herself wasn't enough to raise her suspicions since all the shoes were a jumble but this one was red and didn't seem to have a matching companion. She picked it up and reached inside, withdrawing a wrinkled plastic baggie with just enough crumbly pot in the bottom to form a joint.

Paula's heart sank.

* * *

All day Saturday, Paula fretted about what to do. She left Dale several messages on his cell phone, trying to sound vague and urgent at the same time, before finally getting a voice mail (she was in the bathroom) that he was in Kings Canyon fishing with his buddy Greg and would try her again Sunday night, when he got back. That left Paula pretty much on her own since Michael would return before then.

"If it were my kid I'd whomp him in the face and lock him in his room," offered Alvin Pulley, one of the agents in the office. Alvin, a former chef-turned-commercial-real-estate-broker, weighed over 300 pounds so that seemed like a plausible option for him.

Cora Webb, Windsong's graphic designer, had a different take: "I'd just put it back and pretend like I never noticed," she said. "All kids smoke pot nowadays." That, too, seemed reasonable coming from Cora, a Parson's graduate whom Paula had caught toking up behind the rest room at the company picnic. Her only reaction had been to give Paula a sly smile and hold out the tiny stub of the joint to share. Paula declined.

Meanwhile, Paula tried to compose her letter to Mason J. Sibley, Milo's attorney. She got as far as "Dear Mr. Sibley" before her computer crashed and reset itself. Whenever the desktop would finally stop loading, it would reset again and the process would repeat. Since it was Saturday, she had to page tech support and wait for a call back; they promised to have the problem fixed by the time Paula got back from her open house, but Joey Tombley, the tech guy, was still at her machine when she returned to the office.

"I think you've got a short on your main board," he opined.

"Am I going to lose anything?" she asked.

"I don't think so," Joey said. "But I'm going to have to take this back to the shop to figure out what's going on."

Paula sighed and sat at her empty desk when he had gone, staring at the loose cables. Then she took down a piece of Windsong stationary and started writing, with an ordinary ink pen, "Dear Mr. Sibley..."

By the time she finished, it was after three, and she had to drive her letter directly to the FedEx office near the airport.

* * *

She had left the pot on the kitchen counter, still not sure what to do with it. But when she came in, the baggie was gone, and the house reeked of marijuana smoke. That was when she saw the half-empty milk container on the sink, and Michael's sports bag thrown onto the couch.

He was lying in his darkened room, the iPod in his ears, a pillow over his head. One of her triangular orange ash trays sat on the night stand, and in it, the roach end of a marijuana joint. She yanked the ear plugs out of his ears and threw the pillow across the room.

"Sit up!" she barked.

"I can't," he said.

"Sit up. We're going to have a conversation."

"Yeah right," he said, not moving.

Paula grabbed his arm and tried to jerk him out of bed. He winced and only then did she notice that his right foot was swathed in a bandage.

"What happened?" she asked.

"I got cut," he said.

"Cut how?"

"I fell on a rock."

Paula's anger momentarily morphed into motherly concern. She sat on the edge of the bed and examined the expertly wound bandage.

"How bad is it?" she asked.

"Bad enough. I can't climb anyway. They gave me a shot."

"What kind of a shot?"

"I don't know. Tetanus, I think." He turned away and she felt her anger rising again.

"So you came home and smoked this," she said, waving the roach in front of his face.

"My foot hurt."

"How long have you been smoking pot."

"Not long," Michael said. "How long have you been going through my things?"

He stared at her defiantly and it was all she could do not to apply the Alvin Pulley method of child discipline.

Just then, her cell phone rang. Not knowing where to go next with Michael, she rose from the bed and answered it. It was Chucky Milo, clear as a bell.

"Wow, that's funny," Chucky said, as soon as they had finished their hellos. "This is the best connection yet and we're in the middle of another squall. The web cam's working too."

Her son reached for the roach in the ashtray and Paula slapped it out of his hand. She picked it up from where it had fallen at her feet and made an I'll-deal-with-you-later grimace at Michael. Then she went into the living room so she could concentrate on her conversation with Milo.

"Listen," she said, anxious to conclude their business before the phone went bad again.

"Hold on," Milo said. There was a sound like a wet broom brushing across concrete and some muffled cries. A minute later she heard voices barking in an incomprehensible tongue, more shouting, and then nothing.

Paula threw the phone down in frustration and marched back to Michael's room to finish their conversation.

His bed was empty. He had slipped out the window, pulling the Roman shade off its track in the process.

Paula put the shade on the desk, closed the window, and sat on the edge of her son's bed, where she pinched herself, hard, to avoid crying.

* * *

Paula spent the rest of the evening calling the parents of Michael's friends on the theory that he would eventually turn up at one of their houses. When that yielded no results, she jumped in the car and began checking the places he liked to hang out—the skate park, the high school bleachers, the pizza parlor near the Ralph's. On a hunch, she even drove out to Desert Hot Springs to the canyon where once he'd been picked up in the beer bust. She found a couple in a Toyota making out and a lot of empty beer cans, but no Michael.

Paula tried to think back to her childhood, so prim and sheltered compared to what kids did today. She didn't even know what pot was until she was 20 and in college, and had taken a single puff on a dare so as not to look like the dork she was. Of course, she did have an occasional cocktail and maybe more than one right after the divorce and now she wondered whether seeing his mother drunk could have set Michael off. She did preach to him, and more than once had used the "Do you want to end up flipping burgers" line until he started saying, "Do you want fries with that?" to her every time he got a chance. She knew kids didn't always do what you wanted them to do, but wasn't it your job to protect them from themselves and keep them from doing anything inappropriate?

About midnight, after driving the streets of Palm Springs aimlessly for another hour, she gave up, discouraged, and drove home, half-hoping she'd find Michael safe and sound in bed. His room was empty, however, and the phone was lying on the floor where she had thrown it. She noticed a red light flashing on its corner and picked it up. She had a text message from Michael. "Gone to dadz" it said.

She had no idea how he could have gone to his father when his father lived in San Diego, two hours away, but she was relieved, and soon fell into an exhausted sleep.

* * *

She was awakened at six a.m. by a ringing phone, her home phone this time, on the nightstand beside the bed.

It must be Michael, she thought. He's stuck somewhere and wants me to come get him. But no. It was Steve Coughlin, the L.A. owner of the condo she was trying to sell Milo.

"The deal's still on, you know," were the first words out of his lips. "He signed the contract in the name of Chucky Milo, Inc."

Paula sat up, groggy and confused. First of all, Coughlin shouldn't have been calling her at all since he had his own agent, secondly what difference did it make whether Milo was taking title to the condo personally or in the name of his corporation? And thirdly it was Coughlin's stubbornness with the lease that was holding everything up. But before she could recover he went on, as if reading her mind.

"I'm dropping my objections to renewing the lease. You'll have the papers on your desk Monday," he said.

More awake now, Paula felt indignation rising in her breast. She was tired of dealing with asshole sellers. "This is totally inappropriate," she complained. "Have your agent call me during office hours. How did you get my home number, anyway?"

"I Googled you," he said. "Anyway, I just wanted to let you know, the deal is still on. We have a contract despite this unfortunate business."

"What unfortunate business?"

"You mean you don't even know? What kind of an agent are you? It's all over CNN!"

Paula had had enough of the attorney's cryptic arrogance so she hung up, then threw off the blankets and shuffled over to the TV, where some senator from New England was proposing a two dollar a gallon gasoline tax to fund tuition benefits for children of illegal aliens. It seemed a yawner until Paula noticed her client's name scrolling across the bottom of the screen:

> *Internet mogul Chucky Milo killed by pirates off coast of Indonesia.*

Paula sat on the floor in front of the tube and waited for the news to cycle around so she could get the details of the story. They were not pleasant. Apparently Milo's junk had been attacked by Indonesian pirates, who had swarmed the ship during a storm and hacked to death a number of passengers who resisted, including Milo and super-model Nora Fedyushhyna. Bizarrely, the whole incident had been caught on an infrared web cam Milo had set up on the bridge of the ship. The pirates, in ghostly form, could be seen hanging from the rail of the ship just before boarding and pushing back the passengers to the edge of the camera range. Milo could be seen talking into his satellite phone just before it was knocked out of his hands and he was forced to his knees. CNN declined to broadcast the actual murder, but said he had been stabbed several times in the chest. The remaining passengers had been locked in the hold while the ship was looted.

Paula turned off the TV and dialed Dale's home number. The phone rang three times and then was picked up by the answering machine. She hung up. It wasn't even 6:30 so she couldn't blame Jill, Dale's wife, for not picking up.

Next she tried Michael's cell phone. It, too, rang three times before switching to voice mail. Paula hung up again and took the device to the kitchen table, where, by painfully running through letters on the telephone keys, she was able to laboriously compose and send a text message:

"Call me. Mom."

A few moments later, her phone booped and she picked it up. Michael had texted her back:

"i h8t u."

She thought about it a few minutes, then texted, "I luv U. Call me."

A minute later the phone booped again: "y r u like that?"

She sighed. She could see that, once again, he was going to blame his problems on her, a trick he had undoubtedly picked up from Dale.

"Like what?" she texted.

There was no immediate response. After awhile, Paula got tired of waiting and wandered off to boil an egg.

Only as she was peeling it did she realize Chucky must have been on the phone to her when the pirates attacked. Those were the cries she had heard.

Suddenly the kitchen seemed stuffy and the house very still.

She left her phone on the counter and went outside to the backyard, for some Palm Springs sunlight and air.

———✦———

ABOUT THE AUTHOR

D. G. Voda is a former real estate agent who had the great hindsight to retire from the Palm Springs market just two years after it crashed.

The author left behind an algae-filled pool, a heat-prostrated dog, several overwrought creditors and more than 500 glossy tri-fold sales brochures proclaiming "D. G. Voda, Your Desert Friend."